ABOUT THIS BOOK

CRACKER JACKSON
Betsy Byars

The letter was pink with yellow roses on the flap. There was nothing about it to indicate danger. But when Jackson read the anonymous note, he felt his arms tremble, the paper become heavier. "Keep away, Cracker, or he'll hurt you." The note could mean only one thing. Only Alma called him "Cracker," the nickname she gave him when she first became his babysitter. Now Alma was married, with a child of her own, and she was in trouble. But how could he help? He'd promised Alma not to involve his mother. His father wasn't living at home anymore, and a phone call would be useless. Dad couldn't stop doing Porky Pig imitations long enough for Cracker to talk. That left Goat, his best friend and the class clown. But Goat's schemes were always high on lunacy and low on results. And then there was Alma herself, childlike in her affections and faith, caught up in a situation beyond her control.

"The book belongs in the same distinguished category as *The Summer of the Swans* in its expert blend of humor and compassion."
                                                          —*Horn Book*

Cracker Jackson

Cracker Jackson

BETSY BYARS

Troll Associates

PUFFIN BOOKS

Viking Penguin Inc., 40 West 23rd Street, New York, New York 10010, U.S.A.
Penguin Books Ltd, 27 Wrights Lane, London W8 5TZ (Publishing & Editorial) and
Harmondsworth, Middlesex, England (Distribution & Warehouse)
Penguin Books Australia Ltd, Ringwood, Victoria, Australia
Penguin Books Canada Limited, 2801 John Street, Markham, Ontario, Canada L3R 1B4
Penguin Books (N.Z.) Ltd, 182-190 Wairau Road, Auckland 10, New Zealand

First published by Viking Penguin Inc. 1985
Published in Puffin Books 1986

10 9 8 7 6 5 4

Copyright © Betsy Byars, 1985
All rights reserved
Printed in U.S.A.
Set in Times Roman
Library of Congress Cataloging in Publication Data
Byars, Betsy Cromer.   Cracker Jackson.
Summary: After attempting to save his ex-babysitter from wife abuse,
Cracker Jackson gains an adult insight into the
sadness of failed heroics.
[1. Wife abuse—Fiction]   I. Title.
PZ7.B9836Cr 1986   [Fic]   86-4857   ISBN 0-14-031881-X

Reprinted by arrangement with Viking Penguin,
a division of Penguin Books USA Inc.

Contents

CONTENTS

Cracker Jackson

Anonymous
Letters

"There's a letter for you."

"For me?" Jackson was pleased. He didn't get that much mail. "Where?"

"On the coffee table."

The envelope was pink. There were yellow roses on the flap. His name and address were in pencil. There was nothing to indicate danger.

"Who's it from?" his mother asked.

"Well, let me open it."

He lifted the flap, took out the sheet of paper, and unfolded it. There was only one sentence. He read it and stopped breathing.

Keep away, Cracker, or he'll hurt you.

The letter was not signed.

"So, who is it from?" his mother asked.

He didn't hear her. The sentence was already pounding in his head, echoing . . . *or he'll hurt you . . . hurt you . . . hurt you . . .*

"Jackson?"

"Oh, what?"

"Who's your letter from?"

"Nobody."

"It must be from somebody. Let me see. The handwriting looks familiar."

He folded the letter quickly. "It's from somebody at school," he lied. "You don't know her."

"Her? Well, she must like you if she's writing you letters."

"She might. She's not very bright. She's been held back twice."

He looked down at the envelope, suddenly feeling the weight of the sheet of paper. His elbows began to tremble. It seemed to him then that anonymous letters actually weigh more than normal letters. Or maybe they just weaken the person who gets them. He didn't know. Anyway, this was the second anonymous letter he had gotten in his eleven years of life, and both of them had been heavy enough to make his elbows tremble.

"Anyway, Mom," he said in a voice that was not quite

steady, "there are other reasons for writing people letters than because you like them."

"Oh?" She put down her magazine and slid her glasses up on top of her head.

It was a question, but he did not answer. Suddenly he couldn't remember ever having gotten a letter from someone who liked him. His mail seemed one anonymous letter after another.

His first had been left on his desk after recess in first grade. His name was on the outside. Inside, he remembered, there were two words, and they were in cursive writing. He had poked Marian Wong, who was the class brain.

"Can you read that?"

"Of course."

"What does it say?"

"It says, 'You stink.' "

Marian had turned back to the front of the class and he had sat heavily at his desk, painfully aware that the unfortunate words meant that he, his whole self, he, the center of the universe, not just his armpits or his sweat socks, stank.

"Jackson, your face is red," Miss Riley said. "Were you chasing the preschoolers at recess again?"

"Nome."

"What did I tell you boys about chasing preschoolers?"

"Not to do it!"

"That's right. Where is your reading book, Jackson?"

"I don't know."

"Well, have you looked in your desk?"

"Nome."

As he fumbled in his desk for the book, he glanced around the room to see if anybody was watching his discomfort. Everybody was reading, apparently engrossed in Dick and Jane and their new kitten, Floppy.

He mentally checked off the people who could not have sent the note, who were above such stupidity . . . Marian Wong, Elizabeth Ann Rogers . . . until he was left with six possibilities.

Laboriously he printed six notes. "So do you."

When the noon bell rang for lunch, he was the last person out of the room. This allowed him to drop the notes on the desks of the appropriate suspects—Bubba Riley, Goat McMillan, Willie and Billie Bonsal, Lulu McGee, and Skrunky Cooke.

Five people—Goat, Willie and Billie, Lulu, and Skrunky—came back in, saw their notes. Oho, what is this? A note for me? They read them and looked genuinely puzzled.

Bubba Riley opened his, turned around, looked directly at Jackson, and stuck out his tongue.

So much for anonymous letter writer #1.

"Your nose is running, Jackson," his mother said.

He was still standing by the coffee table, statue-still, his trembling arms pressed against his sides, feeling the increasing weight of the letter. It had to weigh as much as a bowling ball by now. It was actually dragging his arms toward the floor.

"Jackson!"

"Oh, what?"

"Your nose is running!"

"Yeah, I guess it is."

He took a tissue from the box on the coffee table. His nose ran most of the time, so there were boxes of tissue all over the house. But when something happened to make him emotional—like this letter—his nose poured.

He had even started a list of activities that his runny nose made impossible. So far he had only (1) Kissing Girls and (2) Singing Opera, but he knew he would be adding to the list. Like Brain Surgeon, for example—that was out. Imagine saying to the operating nurse, "Scalpel . . . suture . . . clamp . . . Kleenex."

"Are you all right, Jackson?"

"Yes, I'm fine."

He glanced up as if he were not quite sure which way the exit was. Then, holding the tissue over his nose, he headed for the hall.

He walked into his room and stopped in the middle of the braided rug. The circles going out were like circles on a radar screen, warning of danger.

With his free hand he shook the letter open.

Keep away, Cracker, or he'll hurt you.

It was the big, round handwriting of a person who did not do a lot of writing and had to spend time on each letter. He read the sentence a third time, and a fourth. The words did exactly what his English teacher was always saying a sentence should do—form a complete thought.

The letter, too heavy to hold now, fell from his hand and dropped to the floor. He was surprised that it didn't clang like metal as it landed.

Two anonymous letters in one lifetime. It seemed more than a person could bear. The messages were burned into his brain. When he was ninety—if he lived that long—he would still be able to repeat exactly, word for word, both of them. *You stink. Keep away, Cracker, or he'll hurt you.*

At least this time he did not have to set a clever trap to find out who had sent the letter. This time he knew.

Only one person had ever called him Cracker.

Bbbrrruucckkkk

Jackson was still standing in the middle of his braided rug when he heard his mother go into the kitchen to start supper. As if he had been waiting for the sound of the refrigerator door opening, he went down the hall and into his mother's room.

He looked at the phone on her bedside table. For a moment he did not move. He was torn between the need to call and the sure knowledge that it was the worst thing he could do. Of all his choices, this was the most stupid.

He picked up the receiver and held it against his chest. The dial tone droned, then beeped to alert him the phone was off the hook. With his thumb he found the receiver and pushed it. Silence. After a long moment, he sighed and began to push the buttons.

The phone rang. Beneath his breath Jackson said, Don't let him answer. Don't let him answer. Don't let him—

"Jackson!" his mother called from the kitchen.

He slammed down the phone. "What?"

"Do you want pizza or a steak sandwich?"

"I don't care."

"We haven't had pizza in a long time. Is that all right?"

"Pizza's fine."

He waited until he heard the sound of pizza making in the kitchen. He lifted the receiver again. He was breathing in and out now like an athlete readying himself for a feat of strength. Slowly, making sure he had each one right, he pressed the buttons.

The phone began to ring, and Jackson began his ritual. Don't let him answer. Don't let him answer. Don't—

The phone was answered on the fifth ring. A man's voice said, "Billy Ray's garage."

Jackson knew he should hang up, but for some reason he was incapable of doing so. The sound of Billy Ray's voice left him with that paralyzed dread of the prey for his enemy.

"Who *is* this?"

The voice was irritated now. Jackson closed his eyes. He was clutching the phone against his cheek, shoulders hunched, as if he were waiting for a blow.

The voice said, "It's that kid again. I'm going to kill that kid if he—"

And the phone was hung up.

Jackson lowered the receiver and sat on the edge of his mother's bed. The phone rang, and he leaped up. One hand went over his pounding heart.

"I'll get it," his mother called cheerfully from the kitchen. "Hello . . . Yes, he's here . . . Just a minute . . . Jackson, it's for you."

He swallowed. "Who is it?"

"Goat."

Relief swept over him so powerfully that he had to sit down. He took the phone. In a rush he said, "Goat, am I glad it's you! Can you get out after supper? I need you to go somewhere with me."

"I'm grounded. I'm in the closet right now. If my mom knew I was on the phone, she'd—"

"You can get out."

"I can't. She's watching me like a hawk."

"There's a window in your room. You—"

"Not this time, pal. Did you hear what I did?"

"No, but—"

"You didn't hear what me and Percy Gill did in the movie Saturday?" Goat's voice rose with enthusiasm.

Jackson said quickly, "I haven't got much time, Goat, and—"

"You'll love this."

"Goat, I—"

"Me and Percy were in the show—boring movie—singing pirates—and so Percy noticed some girls from our homeroom sitting below the balcony. It was Charmaine and Tara and Tiffany. We go to the water fountain and wet our popcorn and come back to our seats in the front row—we're right above them—and Percy starts making noises like he's going to puke, and then he gives one humongous gag—*BBBRRRUUCCKKKK*—and we dump the wet popcorn over the railing.

"You should have been there. It was like a cattle stampede. Those girls got up screaming and crawling for the aisle—it was worse than if somebody had yelled 'fire!' I'm telling you, pal, when those girls start for the exit, you do not want to be in their way."

"Goat, I—"

"Me and Percy rush down the steps to enjoy the fun, and there was the manager. It was like Gestapo time. He arrested us! Man, he took us by the arms and picked us up bodily and carried us across the lobby—my arm's still sore—to call our moms.

"And my mom, she has zero sense of humor. You know my imitation of the clumsy brain surgeon? You know the one where I use the basketball for the brain? Believe it or not, she saw me do that whole routine and did not smile once. You would have thought she was watching real brain surgery. So then the manager—"

"Goat—"

"I'm just getting to the best part, believe it or not. When

the manager asked my name, like an idiot, I gave it. 'My name is Ralph McMillan. I live at 104 Baker Street.' Only when the manager asks Percy, he says, 'My name is Peter Frampton.' Peter Frampton! The principal's son! It broke me up. The manager says—"

"Goat, will you shut up and listen for a minute?"

"Why? What's happened? Is something wrong?"

"Yes. Remember Alma?"

"Alma? Sure."

"Remember we saw her in McDonald's last Saturday and she had a black eye?"

"Yes."

"Well, I think her husband's beating up on her."

"That was her husband with her? The big guy with the tattoo?"

"Billy Ray. Yeah."

"Pal, you do not want to mess with him. He's bad news. Anybody who has a python tattooed on his arm is—"

"I don't want to mess with him. I just want to ride over there, past their house, and make sure she's all right."

"Take some advice and stay out of it. You're liable to get hurt yourself."

Jackson remembered the letter, the tone of Billy Ray's voice on the phone, his words: *I'm going to kill that kid if he*— "That is a real possibility," he said.

"So let me finish about Percy—" Goat broke off abruptly and Jackson heard him say, "Mom, we're talking about an English assignment. Jackson and I are—"

The phone was hung up, and Jackson went into the kitchen. His mother was taking the pizza out of the oven. Jackson's half was cheese and sausage and tomato sauce; his mom's was chopped tomatoes, bean sprouts, and black olives.

"Goat and I are going to ride bicycles after supper," he said as he pulled out his chair.

His mother watched him over her bean sprouts. "Be home before dark."

"Mom, no driver is going to hit me. My bike glows like a neon sign."

Jackson had the only Day-Glo bike in the county. Other kids had Day-Glo strips on their fenders, but Jackson's whole bike glowed. Still, his mom worried that a motorist wouldn't see him.

"Jackson Hunter, you promise to be home before dark, or you are not leaving the house."

"I promise," he said instantly.

He took a bite of pizza before it was cool, and it burned the roof of his mouth. As he soothed the burn with milk, he thought of all the hundreds of promises he had made over the years.

"You cannot go outside until you promise you won't put any more rocks up your nose." (Sure, I was going to try acorns next anyway.)

"I don't care if everybody in the neighborhood is allowed to ride their trikes in the street, you have to promise you won't." (Sure, but you didn't say no riding on the railroad tracks!)

"Remember," his mother said, breaking into his thoughts, "your father calls tonight. It's Thursday."

Jackson swallowed his milk. "I never forget that," he said.

Wrong Worries,
Right Worries

"Please don't call ɪɪɪm Cracker." Jackson could remember the exact day his mother had said that to Alma.

"What, Miz Hunter?"

"Don't call him Cracker."

"Oh, I don't."

"You just did it."

"I mean, I don't out in public. It's just a pet name. I call him that because, to me, he's like a box of Cracker Jack—real sweet with a surprise inside, like, you know, in a box of Cracker Jack you always get a little prize or a toy or a decal you can paste on yourself? Well, that's what he reminds me of—real sweet, but always coming up with a surprise, like the other day he said . . . " Alma had trailed off, sensing that her explanation was not going over. "I won't call him Cracker anymore, Miz Hunter, if you don't want me to."

"I hate nicknames," his mother had said.

"Oh, me, too. My little sister used to not be able to say Alma and she'd call me Lama and—"

"My greatest fear is that when he goes to school the kids are going to call him Jackie."

"They won't, Miz Hunter, not if you send a note to the teacher."

Jackson realized now that his mother had wasted a large portion of her life worrying about the wrong things happening to him, like kids calling him Jackie, or people putting razor blades and needles in his trick-or-treat candy, or getting a disease from a rest room. Tonight, right now, she was worrying that he would get hit by a car in the dark, and here he was pedaling to Alma's and only that afternoon Alma had sent him a letter saying, Keep away, Cracker, or you'll be hurt, and Billy Ray had threatened murder.

Jackson paused at the intersection and waited for the light to change. Of course, to be fair, he admitted his mother had had certain fears for him that had happened. She had worried that his nose would never stop running, and it never had. She had worried that Goat would come to his piano recital, sit in the front row, and break him up during "The Parade of the Little White Mice," and he had.

The light changed and Jackson pedaled through the intersection. His mother had worried that he would do something crude at his great-grandmother's birthday party, and he had. Inexplicably, he had licked the salt shaker. He had been passing the salt shaker to Great-grandmother and he had licked it.

To this day, he didn't know what had made him do that. He had never licked a salt shaker before. He never planned to lick another.

"What possessed you?" his mother had asked on the way home.

"I dunno."

"Why would anybody in their right mind lick a salt shaker? Why? Why? Why?"

Every time she asked, "Why?" she hit the horn. Other motorists started staring at them.

"I dunno," he kept answering, but that only increased her anger.

It had seemed to him as he sat there, rigid with shame and a tight seat belt, that "Why?" was the most impossible question a person was ever asked.

Once Goat had asked, "Why do you care about Alma? She's not a relative, is she?"

"No."

"Then why do you care?"

"I can't help it," he had answered, a switch on the old

"I dunno," but Goat had nodded with instant sympathy. "Oh," he had said. That was the difference between friendship and authority, that understanding "Oh."

His thoughts broke off as he turned the corner of Alma's street. Her house, set back from the road, was dark. The windows were closed.

Jackson crossed the street and pedaled slowly down the opposite sidewalk, keeping close to the shrubbery. He stopped behind some overgrown azaleas.

Alma and Billy Ray lived next door to Billy Ray's garage. Alma used to bring Jackson here to play when she was baby-sitting. His first feeling of accomplishment had come from handing tools to Billy Ray. "This one?"

"No, the Phillips-head screwdriver."

"This one?"

"Yeah, now you're getting smart."

Jackson waited, clutching the handlebars, ready for a quick getaway. After a moment he saw movement on the porch. The front door was opening. He pressed back deep into the azaleas. His nose began to run.

Alma came out onto the porch. She was holding her baby, Nicole. Nicole had been named for Alma's favorite soap-opera character. Jackson had learned this one afternoon when he was looking through the scrapbook Alma had made about Nicole.

> Height at birth: 22 inches
> Weight at birth: 7 pounds, 10 ounces
> Color of hair: gold

Color of eyes: sky blue
Named for: Nicole on *All My Children*

Alma sat down in the swing.

Jackson lowered his bike to the ground. He could see that Billy Ray's truck was not in the driveway and the doors to the garage were closed.

Jackson slipped across the street and up to the porch railing. Face against the railing, he said, "Hi."

"Cracker." The sound of her voice made it a reproach. "You know you are not supposed to be here."

"I had to come. I was worried about you."

"If Billy Ray finds out . . ."

Jackson glanced quickly over his shoulder. "Where is he? His truck's gone. Isn't he—"

"He's over at his mom's, fixing the fridge."

"Then we're all right."

"No, we aren't, Cracker. Billy Ray could come home at any minute, and he's gotten so he doesn't like you hanging around here. Did you hear what he said on the phone tonight? He knew that was you. He said—"

"I heard, but I'm worried about you."

"Why? I'm fine."

"You always have bruises."

"I have real delicate skin. I've been like that all my life. I bruise if anybody looks at me hard."

"I never used to see bruises on you, not until you got married."

"You just didn't notice." She set the swing in motion and said to Nicole, "There's Cracker down in the bushes. You see Cracker, Pop Tart?"

Nicole was six months old. She was looking up at a moth on the ceiling, not paying any attention to the face in the bushes. Her fingers curled around the hem of Alma's sleeve.

In a lower voice Alma said, "Billy Ray does not beat up on me, if that's what you're thinking."

"I just can't see how you could get so many bruises. Your eye's still black."

"I told you about that. I bumped into a door. I got up in the middle of the night to go to the bathroom and bumped into a door."

"I don't believe you."

"Nicole heard me, didn't you, Sunshine?" She leaned down and kissed Nicole's forehead. She used to do that to Jackson when he was little, and he could still remember how nice it felt.

There was a silence, and then Alma looked at him. "You didn't tell your mama, did you, about my black eye?"

"No."

"Promise me you won't." She kept looking at him. Then she said again, forcefully for her, "Promise."

He knew that Alma cared a lot about what his mother thought of her. At one time she even wanted to be a stewardess like his mom, flying to Chicago and San Francisco and other far places, pulling matched luggage on wheels behind her, not a hair out of place, her dark glasses set stylishly on her head.

He knew that his mother's color-coordinated outfits were, to Alma, the height of fashion. Jackson had once found Alma trying on one of his mother's stewardess outfits. She was holding the jacket shut with her hands because it was too small. "Oh, Cracker," she said when she saw him in the doorway, "do you think I'll ever be thin enough to be a stewardess?"

His answer had been immediate and honest. "Yes."

"I don't know." She had looked at herself sideways. "Maybe if I went to jazzercise."

Now there was a pause, with only the creaking of the porch swing to break the silence. Then Jackson said, "I got your letter telling me not to come."

"Well, it must not have made much of an impression on you. Here you are."

"Why did you say I would be hurt?" The words burst out. Suddenly he was leaning forward like a public defender with a reluctant witness. "Why did you say that, if Billy Ray doesn't hurt people?"

"I didn't say he didn't hurt people, Cracker. Billy Ray is a fighter. He's got his daddy's temper. But he wouldn't hit me or the baby, and he wouldn't hit you either unless your being around here got on his nerves so bad he couldn't help himself. I don't want you to come anymore."

"I like to come. I feel like this is my home."

"And I like having you, only it just can't be."

"He used to not mind my coming."

"That's when I was baby-sitting. Anyway, it's Billy Ray's house, Cracker. He makes the payments. He decides who— Oh, Lord, there's his pickup!"

"Where?"

"Get down, Cracker. Don't let him see you. Please! Get down!"

From the Bushes

Jackson fell to his knees in the bushes. He cowered, shivering suddenly in the heat. Through the leaves he watched Billy Ray's blue pickup truck turn into the driveway. Its oversized tires threw gravel onto the straggly lawn.

The truck stopped by the side of the porch, ten feet from where Jackson knelt in the dirt. He closed his eyes and breathed through his mouth. His breath sounded ragged, loud in the sudden stillness, and he cupped his hands over his face to muffle the sound.

His hands smelled of sweat and fear. His nose began to run.

Don't let him see me . . . Don't let him see me . . . Please don't let him—

He heard Alma get up off the swing and walk to the side of the porch. The empty swing rocked crazily on its chains.

"Hi. You're home early," she said. Her voice sounded normal, as if she were genuinely glad to see him. There was no trace of the panic that had sent Jackson trembling to his knees. "I wasn't expecting you till nine or ten."

Jackson's nose was running like a faucet. As usual, he did not have a tissue. He wiped it on his pants leg.

"Never wipe your nose on your clothes," his mother had told him once, preparing him for life in a social world. "Never blow your nose on a napkin. Even if it's a paper napkin, you should . . . " "Jackson, never put silverware in your ear. If your ear itches, wait until you leave the table and then . . ."

She had prepared him perfectly for that mannerly world of ladies and gentlemen who would be turned off by the misuse of napkins and forks, by bodily noises, by talking with the mouth full. "No one wants to see what you are chewing, Jackson, and if you laugh with your mouth full, you will . . ."

"Never lick the side of your hamburger bun, Jackson, if you see the ketchup's going to drip, you . . . " "Never spit on yourself, Jackson. If there's a spot on your arm, go into the bathroom and wash your whole arm . . ."

Nothing she had ever taught him had prepared him for

the world he was in right now, where he knelt shivering with fear in the dirt, praying for deliverance.

The conversation sounded so normal at the end of the porch that Jackson lifted his head. He peered over the edge of the porch like a child too little to reach the table.

He could not see Billy Ray's face, only his large, squarish hands on the steering wheel. Alma had shifted Nicole to her hip and was patting her back with her multiringed hand.

Suddenly Jackson remembered an old story his father used to read to him. "Fee—fi—fo—fum," his father would cry in a voice loud enough to actually belong to a giant, "I smell the blood of an Englishman!"

Jackson had trembled then with the knowledge that a giant could actually smell a stranger. He trembled now with the knowledge that Billy Ray had the same awful sense of smell.

Maybe Billy Ray hadn't seen the glow of his bike, maybe he hadn't seen the leaves of the bushes tremble, maybe he hadn't heard the gasps for breath, but he had surely smelled a stranger.

Jackson shuddered. He could taste the pizza he'd eaten for supper.

"There wasn't anything wrong with the fridge, except that little Luther had stuck a screwdriver in the controls," Billy Ray said. His voice sounded normal, too.

Alma laughed. "He's your nephew—mechanically minded." The only thing that betrayed her nervousness was her hand, awkwardly patting Nicole's back again and again.

"Mama would have knocked me cold if I'd done something like that when I was little. She'll let Luther do anything."

"That's a grandmother for you. Listen, go on around back. I want to show you something. I've found the perfect spot for Nicole's jungle gym."

"Bring me a beer, babe."

"It's on the way."

As soon as the pickup disappeared around the house, Jackson got up and crawled through the bushes. The leaves plucked at his clothes, held him back, like in Disney movies when trees and bushes come to life and grow fingers and arms. He struggled to his feet.

He started running. He ran the way soldiers run under fire, zigzagging across the sparse lawn, prepared at any moment to fall to his stomach and bury his head under his arms.

It was not yet dark, but Jackson could see that his bike had already started to glow in the pre-dusk shade of the azaleas. He hoped Billy Ray hadn't seen that glow because Billy Ray knew Jackson had the only Day-Glo bike in the county. Once he'd said, "I'm going to make a neon pretzel out of that bike if I see it around here one more time."

Jackson grabbed his bike, threw one leg over, and came out of the azaleas like a cannonball. In a shower of torn leaves and twigs, he started pedaling fast for home.

Fears and Leeches

Jackson's head was lowered over the handlebars of his bicycle. He was still pedaling fast, four blocks from Alma's house. He had never once dared to look behind him. Now, at Elm Street, he stopped for a red light. He glanced around. No blue pickup truck in sight. No Billy Ray.

Jackson rested against his bicycle seat and tried to catch his breath.

His mother had once told him that some people are especially sensitive to cold, they feel cold more than other people. Some people are more sensitive to pain. Some to pollen.

His own special sensitivity, he realized now, was to fear.

He felt fear so strongly that it actually chilled him to the bone, made his body tremble.

In school one time, Jackson's class had to write compositions on their earliest memories. Marian Wong's earliest memory was from age two, when she surprised her aunt by reading an ad in the evening newspaper. Goat's was locking himself in the bathroom and his mother could not get the door open and he thought he would be in there for the rest of his life, so he painted a mural on the wallpaper with toothpaste and shaving cream and when his mother finally got the door open she spanked him and shut him up in the bathroom again for punishment.

Jackson's earliest memory was of fear.

Alma, his new baby-sitter, had taken him down to the creek behind the apartment house to wade. He was five years old but he had never been allowed to wade before, and stomping around in muddy water made him happier than he had known it was possible to be.

When he and Alma got out of the creek, they noticed there were some brown things on their ankles. Jackson was pleased, and Alma was, too.

"What are they, Cracker? Mine don't want to come off, do yours?"

Jackson was delighted to report his didn't want to come off, either.

They admired them for a short while and then ran to the apartment to show them to Nicholas, Jackson's friend, before they fell off.

"Nicholas won't have any!" Alma cried, and Jackson charged up the hill, his puny legs pumping with unexpected iron.

Jackson's mother surprised them as they crossed the parking lot. She took one look at their feet and cried, "Leeches!"

Alma was puzzled by Mrs. Hunter's cry of horror.

"What are leeches, Miz Hunter?"

Jackson's mother was too busy looking for a sharp stick to answer. Suddenly Jackson knew his first cold, all-the-way-to-the-bone touch of fear.

He had known from his mother's initial cry that leeches were definitely not a good thing to have on your ankles, and he looked at them now through his tears. The dark, widening, narrowing bands on his pale ankles pulsed with danger.

He began choking on his sobs like someone having a fit, his body rigid with fear, but his mother was too busy prying off his leeches to notice. Alma had her own sharp stick and was working on her own leeches. She was crying, too.

"I told you not to take him to the creek," Jackson's mother said to Alma.

"Nome."

"Well, it was on the list I gave you."

"I lost my list. I dropped my pocketbook getting on the bus and everything fell out and the bus driver wouldn't wait for me to pick them up."

"I won't need you any more today," his mother said to Alma in a cold voice.

"Will you want me tomorrow?"

Tears were still rolling down Alma's cheeks because she needed the job. Alma had more than forty dollars' worth of layaways at Sky City.

"I'll let you know."

"All right, Miz Hunter. Bye-bye, Cracker." Their tears mingled as she kissed his cheek. "I had a real good time sitting for you. Bye, Miz Hunter."

"Good-bye, Alma."

"Is Alma coming back?" Jackson asked as he and his mother went up the stairs.

The leech danger had passed. He now had on his high-top, orthopedic, Stride-Rite shoes, laced tight. He was safe.

"Is she?" Alma was his newest, youngest, and already his favorite baby-sitter.

The only answer his mother would give was the one he hated most: "We'll see."

His mother did let Alma come back, but Alma was never at ease with his mother after that.

Alma was always saying things like "Oh, Gumdrop, I wish I could take you to my boyfriend's garage. There's tires to play in, and you could fingerpaint in the grease pan. And there's a Coke machine and a peanut machine. You put in a penny and you get a handful of peanuts. But I guess I can't. If your mother found out we went to the garage, she wouldn't let me come back."

She had to say it several times before Jackson caught on. Finally he said what Alma was waiting to hear: "She won't find out."

The
Thursday Call

"Did Dad call?"

"No. You're out of breath, Jackson."

"I know."

"It's not good to ride so fast. When I told you to be home before dark, I didn't mean for you to—"

"I wasn't."

He went into his mother's room and lay down on the bed to wait for his father's telephone call. Since his parents got divorced three years ago and his dad moved to L.A., his dad had called Jackson every Thursday night at exactly nine o'clock. He had never once missed calling, and Jackson had never once missed picking up the phone on the first ring.

To his friends, Jackson pretended not to know the reason for his parents' divorce. If he had told them the real reason, they would not have believed him. Jackson's mother had divorced his father because he would not ever, under any circumstances, be serious. Two other women had also divorced him, apparently for the same reason.

Like, if Jackson's mom said something like "Don't wipe your nose on your clothes, Jackson," his dad would say, "That's right, Jackson, wipe it on somebody else's clothes," and he would grab a perfect stranger's coat sleeve and say, "Here you go, son."

Even when something was serious—like the time his mom heard a rumor that Eastern was going to lay off a hundred stewardesses. His mom was very upset. She was crying. "I don't want to get another job. I love what I do. Flying means everything to me."

And Jackson's dad started pretending to be John Wayne. He said, "If—flying—means—that—much—to—you, little—lady"—he sounded more like John Wayne than John Wayne—"then—you—better—start—learning—to—flap—your—arms."

Jackson's earliest memory of his dad was of his not being serious.

He and his father were sitting on the sofa. His father was reading "The Three Bears," only he wouldn't read it right. He didn't have the Mama Bear say, "Somebody's been eating my porridge"; he had her say, "Somebody's been eating my low-fat yogurt."

"No! *Porridge!*" Jackson yelled. He must have been up on this story because he was as upset as if his dad were taking liberties with the Bible. He grabbed his dad's lips and tried to force them to say "Porridge."

His dad was laughing too hard. "Por—por—" More laughter. "Por—por—*porridge!*"

Jackson released his lips, but he sat up straight at his side, as alert as a soldier. The story was still not safe. His father read correctly for a few minutes.

"So, the Papa Bear says, 'Somebody's been sleeping on my bed.' And the Mama Bear says, 'Somebody's been sleeping on my Serta Perfect-Sleeper,' and the—"

"No! Bed! Say *bed!*"

"B-b-b—" More laughter. "Give me a chance! I'll say it! I'll say it! I promise. Let my lips go. *Bed!*"

And so it went. One of the reasons Jackson got bored during reading at school was that the teachers read correctly. His father had never read a story right in his life.

"I think I can, but I'm not motivated. I think I can, but I'm not . . . Rapunzel, Rapunzel, let down your Miss Clairol–treated . . . Gretel, peep into my microwave . . . And I'll huff and I'll puff and I'll blow your double-wide, color-coordinated mobile home down . . . Who will help me eat the vitamin-enriched sourdough from Francisco?"

The phone rang, and Jackson picked it up. A voice said,

"This is the President speaking to you from the Oval Office. Tonight I'd like to talk to you about a matter of concern to all Americans—aardvarks."

Jackson said, "Hi, Dad."

"How did you know it was me?"

"I already talked to the President tonight."

"I should have known. So, how's it going?"

"All right."

"How's school?"

"Fine."

"You and Goat behaving yourselves?"

"No."

"That's good. I don't want any son of mine behaving himself." He began to sound like Dracula. "There are vays to keep people from behaving themselves, and I vill use these vays if necessary." He laughed and then went back to his own voice. "So, what have you been up to?"

"Nothing. Oh, one thing happened. Do you remember a baby-sitter I had, named Alma?"

"Not that big Swedish woman who didn't like me? Misterr Hunterrr, git out off my kitchinn beforre I hit you overrr the head with the skillllet."

"No, that was Anna. Alma was my summer baby-sitter for four years."

"I remember Alma." His voice got slow, Southern. "Jackson, why you sweet-potato casserole, you little gumdrop, you sugar-coated corn pone, you—"

He sounded enough like Alma to make Jackson interrupt sharply, "Don't do that."

"What?"

"Imitate Alma."

"Why not? You let me imitate the President, the Queen of England, Mister Rogers."

"That's different."

"How?"

"Alma's in trouble."

"What kind of trouble?"

"I don't know exactly. I think her husband's beating her up."

Now that he had spoken the terrible words at last, his worries began to pour out. He could not have stopped himself if he'd tried.

"I saw her in McDonald's last week and she had a black eye, and I was over at her house the week before and caught her putting ice on her lip. It was swollen bad. And tonight I went over there and—"

"You went to her house?"

"Yes, and her eye was still black and today she sent me a letter saying to keep away or he'd hurt me and—"

"What are you doing going to her house? If he's beating his wife, he's not going to hesitate about hitting you. Let me talk to your mother."

For the first time in Jackson's memory, his father sounded serious. He said, "Dad, wait a minute. Listen—"

"I want to speak to your mother. Does she know about this?"

"No, and I promised Alma I wouldn't tell her. Alma doesn't want Mom to know."

"Let me speak to your mother."

Jackson glanced up. His mother was standing in the doorway, looking concerned. She had heard him yelling at his father, something he had never done before in all their hundreds of phone calls.

He put his hand over the phone. "Nothing's wrong, Mom. Go back in the living room."

It was an unwritten rule that he got to have private talks with his father.

"Let me speak to your father."

"Mom, this is my call!"

On the phone his father was yelling, "Jackson, I want to speak to your mother. Call your mother to the phone this instant!"

His mother and father were closing the gap, drawing together for strength like strangers with a common trouble. His mother came into the room. She held out her hand.

Jackson hesitated and sighed. Shoulders sagging, he handed her the phone.

Thpitting

"This is the first time in my life I have known your father to be angry."

Jackson's mother was sitting on the sofa. The magazine she had been reading before the phone call was closed. The diet drink she had been drinking was now pale, diluted with melted ice cubes.

"Me, too."

"I didn't even know he was capable of anger."

"I didn't, either."

"All the years we were married, he never got angry one single time. I used to actually try and make him angry. And all it took was for him to get worried about you."

"I guess."

His mother sighed. "I guess he knows wives are re-placeable and you aren't."

"Mom!"

"Well, it's true. You'll always be his only child. I hon-estly believe that if Billy Ray had harmed one hair on your head, your father would have come home and killed him."

"Oh, Mom."

"I do. I had no idea the man could get so angry. He was like a wild man."

"I seem to have a talent for making people angry."

"That's ridiculous, Jackson."

"But true."

Even his mother, whose stewardess training kept her from ever losing her temper with a passenger, could be turned into a raging maniac by his most innocent action. The first time it had happened, Jackson had just started nursery school—Kids Academy. He had been there maybe a week when the teacher, Miss Peggy, pinned a note to his overalls for him to take home.

His mother unpinned the note, read it, and exploded. "Spitting! Since when have you started spitting?"

Jackson stood, nose running, mouth hanging open—he breathed through his mouth a lot—staring up at her.

"Jackson, have you been spitting?"

"Yeth."

"On the floor?"

So that was it. She was afraid he had been spitting on the floor. Even at age three he understood what a serious breach of good manners she would consider this. Proudly he shook his head. Not to worry. He knew better than that. He had not been spitting on the floor.

"On what, then?"

He hesitated. Most of his targets had been fellow students whose names he did not know. He searched his memory for at least one name to please his mother. He came up with one.

"Mith Peggy."

"You spit on Miss Peggy? You spit on your teacher?"

"Yeth."

Actually, this was not quite the truth. The truth was that he spit *at* Miss Peggy. He would take one step forward in his Stride-Rite orthopedic shoes, lean back, and then sort of throw the top half of his body forward and spit. All too frequently he was his own target—but why disturb his mother by mentioning that?

"Why? Why do you do these things, Jackson?"

"I dunno."

"Did you learn this from someone at Kids Academy?"

He shook his head.

"Does anybody else at nursery school spit?"

Again he shook his head. So far as he knew, he was the first person in the history of Kids Academy to spit. However, it was becoming increasingly obvious that instead of being pleased with his originality, his mother was becoming more furious by the minute.

"Then where did you get the idea? Did you see something on television?"

"No."

"Then where did you get the idea?"

"From Billy Frog."

"Who is Billy Frog?"

"In the thtory."

"What story? A book?"

More head shaking.

"Then what story?"

"Daddy thtory."

"Your father has been reading you stories about somebody named Billy Frog who spits on people?"

"No. No. *No!*"

All this was too much emotion, too much anger, too much confusion. He began to cry.

"Billy Frog didn't thpit on people! He thpit on other frogth, frogth he didn't like!"

Instead of being calmed by his explanation, his mother got angrier. "This is your father's fault. I can tell you one thing, young man, there are going to be no more Billy Frog stories!"

Now he began sobbing. His eyes, his nose poured. He loved Billy Frog. He wanted to be just like him. Billy Frog could spit with such force and accuracy that he never missed. Billy Frog had a windup like a baseball pitcher's, and his spit was so fast you couldn't see it, only hear it, because as it struck there was always this sound—*ping!*

Jackson's dream was to stand in Kids Academy, give that fabulous windup, say, "Oh, Mith Peggy." "Yes, what is it, Jackson?" *Ping*!

Jackson was so engrossed in his memories of Billy Frog that his mother had to call his name twice to get his attention.

"Oh, I was thinking about something else, Mom. What did you say?"

"I said maybe I should go over and talk to Alma."

She had his complete attention now. "No, Mom, no! Promise you won't."

"I won't say you told me. Actually, I've been wanting to see the baby. It would be natural for me to—"

"No, she'd know, Mom, please. I promised I wouldn't tell you. She doesn't want you to know. Anyway, she'd just deny it."

"Well, if it's true, there are places she could go. She doesn't have to take his abuse. There's a place in Avondale. I read about it in the paper the other night. Unfortunately, she's not the only wife in the community who's being abused."

He decided to back off. "Maybe she's not being abused. I don't know. She says she's not. Maybe I'm imagining the whole thing. Can we just drop it, please?"

"We can drop it if you promise me you are not going over there anymore. I mean it, Jackson. Your going over there cannot possibly help the situation and may even aggravate it."

The phone rang then, saving him. His mother sighed.

"That's probably your father again. You answer it, Jackson."

"Sure."

He didn't bother going into his mother's room for privacy, because he, too, thought it would be his dad. Instead, it was Goat.

"I can't talk loud," Goat said. "I'm in the closet again. I just wanted to know if you went over there."

Jackson was glad to hear a friendly voice. It had been that kind of night. "Yes."

"Is it your father?" his mom asked.

"No," he said, and she got up and went into the kitchen.

"So, did anything happen?" Goat asked.

"Not really."

"Then why do you sound depressed?"

"I don't know. I'm afraid Billy Ray might have seen my bike."

"Might have? Your bike is like a neon sign, Jack. Didn't you hide it?"

"Yes, behind some bushes, but I could see it when I was running across the yard, and I'm afraid he could, too."

"So he saw it. What's the big deal?"

"I'm afraid he might, you know, take it out on Alma."

"I didn't think of that. Listen, I got an idea. I'll go to her house tomorrow and pretend to be collecting for UNICEF. My sister's a collector for our block, so she's got all the official stuff—can, badge, everything. I can borrow it—she'll never know."

"What good would that do?"

"Well, at least I can get a look at her, make sure she's all right. That's what you wanted, wasn't it? Next week I can pretend to be something else."

Jackson closed his eyes. Gratitude for Goat's friendship washed over him like a warm wave. "Thanks, Goat."

"Don't mention it. I didn't have anything interesting to do tomorrow, anyway."

A Friend Called Goat

One time in science class, Goat got everybody to agree that when the teacher, Mr. Fellini, came back into the room, they would move their lips like they were answering his questions, only they wouldn't make any sound. That way, Goat said, Mr. Fellini would think he was going crazy and would go to the infirmary, leaving them free to have an extra recess.

After Goat explained the plan, he looked at everybody very seriously—his "Winston Churchill Look," he called it. He looked especially long and hard at Marian Wong, who thought school was strictly for learning.

"If anybody speaks," he said, "everyone in the room gets to throw things at him, or"—another serious glance at Marian—"her. Okay?"

Every single person agreed.

Mr. Fellini came back into the room, and when he saw them all sitting there, not talking or making any noise, he said, "Am I in the right room?"

He looked back at the number on the door. "This must be the place." Then he shook his head as if he couldn't believe it.

No one in the class spoke.

Mr. Fellini sat down. "We'll start with the review questions," he said. "Let's see. What do you know about cumulus clouds—mmmmm . . ." He looked around the room, deciding whom to call on. No one breathed. "Mmmm, Marian."

Marian Wong swallowed hard. Everybody thought she was getting ready to speak. She did not. She told everything she knew about cumulus clouds, which happened to be everything in the book and the school encyclopedia, and she never made a sound.

"I can't hear you, Marian. Speak up."

If it had been anybody but Marian, Mr. Fellini would have been suspicious right away. Marian repeated a short summary of her knowledge on cumulus clouds without a sound.

Mr. Fellini said, "Archie, do you think you could give me the answer a little louder?"

Archie had never known the answer to a science question in his life, so he was happy to move his lips and not speak.

Now Mr. Fellini caught on. He must have thought it was Jackson's idea, because Jackson got the next question. Only this time Mr. Fellini didn't make a sound, either, just moved his lips. It gave Jackson a weird feeling. He couldn't even tell what the question was. Without making a sound, however, he answered one about lightning.

Mr. Fellini shook his head. Wrong, he said, opening his mouth wide to show how far off the answer had been. He made a mark beside Jackson's name in his book. He looked up, and his eyes fell on Goat.

"Ralph?"

Goat began moving his lips, answering the question, and then all of a sudden he jumped up out of his seat.

"I can't stand it! I can't stand it! I know it was my idea, but it's driving me crazy instead of Mr. Fellini!"

Everybody picked up books and pencils and threw them at Goat, and he covered his head for protection until they were through. Then he stood up, bowed at the waist, and said, "Thank you for not throwing encyclopedias."

Jackson felt he could spend hours making a list of all the things Goat had done over the years to make him laugh, to make his life happier, but that was not the important thing. Goat was the best, most loyal friend a person could have.

After school Goat got the UNICEF can from his locker—

it had a slit in the top for coins—and a badge that said I Care About Unicef.

He pinned the badge onto his shirt. "How do I look?"

"Official."

"That's how I feel, too."

They walked out of school and in the direction of Alma's house. Goat said, "It's amazing how a badge can give a person a feeling of importance."

He offered his UNICEF can to a passing lady, but she shook her head. "I've already given."

"Thank you, anyway," Goat said cheerfully. "You know, I like to do this. I think I'll be a panhandler when I grow up. Excuse me, sir, would you care to contribute to UNICEF?"

They kept walking for about a mile. Goat collected fourteen cents on the way, and then Jackson stiffened suddenly. "There it is," he said. "That's the garage."

They pulled back out of sight.

Goat said, "Here, hold my books and I'll go the rest of the way by myself. I'll hit a few other houses so it'll look legit."

Jackson stood in the shadows and watched him walk down the sidewalk. Goat turned up at the first house and rang the bell. He waited for a few minutes; then he looked in Jackson's direction, shrugged, and headed for the next house. Nobody was home there, either.

Next was the garage. BILLY RAY ALTON'S GARAGE—COMPLETE OVERHAULS, BODY REPAIRS, PAINT JOBS, FREE ESTI-

MATES. YOU DENT'UM—I FIX'UM, the sign said. Billy Ray had painted the sign himself, with Alma and Jackson watching. Both of them had admired the results, Alma so much that she had said, "If you ever give up the garage, Billy Ray, you can go into sign painting."

The garage was set back from the street, but Goat gave it a wide berth, anyway. He turned in at Alma's house and went up the walk in a brisk, businesslike way. The few coins in the can rattled, announcing his approach. He rang the doorbell.

Jackson could see that someone had opened the door, but he could not see if it was Alma. He waited. His nose started running and he wiped it on his sleeve.

Hours seemed to pass. Jackson tried to imagine what was taking so long. Goat was still standing on the porch, talking. Then, finally, to Jackson's relief, he held out the can and a hand—Alma's—dropped in some coins.

Goat came back down the sidewalk without his usual bounce. His UNICEF can was dangling at his side. Jackson knew instantly that something had gone wrong, and he went forward a few steps to meet Goat—in his concern, leaving the shelter of the bushes. He had never seen Goat walk so slowly.

"Come on!" he hissed. Then, when Goat got within speaking range, he said, "What happened?"

"Bad news, pal," Goat said.

"What? Tell me."

"She looked terrible. Big red swollen place on her face.

Here." He touched his cheek. "Another one here." He touched his jaw.

Jackson suddenly felt sick with alarm. "Did you say anything about it?"

"I felt like I had to. It was very obvious. I said, 'Wow, lady, you must have been in a car wreck.' She said, 'Yes, and I hope I'm never in another one.' "

"It was no car wreck."

"I knew that, but I thought it was better to pretend. I said, 'You ought to always buckle your seat belt.' She said, 'I'm sure going to do that from now on. I've learned my lesson.'

"Then she looked at me for a minute and said, 'Aren't you friends with Jackson Hunter?' I said, 'Jackson who?' She said, 'Don't try to fool me. You were in McDonald's with him the other night.' She remembered me."

"I forgot about that," Jackson said.

"Me, too. Then she said, 'Did Jackson send you over here to check on me?' And I said, 'No, ma'am. I'm collecting for UNICEF. This is my official neighborhood.' I held up my can.

"She looked at the can and that convinced her. She said, 'UNICEF—that's the little foreign children, isn't it?' I said that it was. She said, 'I always feel so sorry for them because they all have such big, sad eyes. Let me see if I've got any change.' Then she went back in the living room and got her purse.

"She came back and said, 'I wish I could give more,

but this is all the change I have.' She gave me a dime and a nickel. I said, 'Every little bit helps. You've given more than a lot of people.' "

"Was that all?" Jackson asked.

Goat shook his head. "She started to close the door, and then she opened it again. She said, 'Will you do me a favor?'

"I said, 'Sure, if I can.'

"She said, 'Don't tell Jackson you saw me.'

"I said, 'I won't if you don't want me to.'

"She said, 'I'd really appreciate it.' Then she shut the door and I walked back here."

Goat and Jackson stood on the sidewalk without moving for a minute. Goat's nose had started running, too. He felt as bad as Jackson. He said, "I wish I hadn't done that—taken her money. I mean, I'm going to give it to my sister and everything, but I just wish I hadn't done it. She was so nice."

Jackson wiped his nose on his sleeve again. "She always has been," he said.

Jackson and
Superman

The phone rang in the middle of *Superman II*. Superman and Lois Lane were making out at the North Pole. Since this was one of Jackson's least favorite parts of the movie, he clicked off the sound and picked up the phone.

"Hello."

"I am in deep trouble."

"What happened, Goat?" Jackson lay back, relaxed, on the sofa. Goat was in deep trouble a lot of the time.

"A friend of my sister's saw me with her UNICEF badge and can, collecting money on the way to Alma's."

Jackson sat up, his spine stiff with alarm. "You didn't tell your sister about Alma, did you?"

"I'm no fink. You know that."

"What'd you tell her?"

"Actually, I told my sister the only thing she would believe. I told my sister that I was ripping people off, collecting money so I could go to the movie on Saturday."

"I appreciate that a lot, Goat. I hope she didn't tell your mom."

"Not yet. So far she's been holding it over my head, making me do stuff for her. You know how she is. Tonight I had to make a tossed salad. Then she got mad because I didn't scrape the carrots. She even tried to make me peel those tiny little tomatoes."

Jackson thought the situation over and said, "That's not so bad. It's not deep trouble, Goat, not in comparison to some of the other trouble you've been in."

"That was just the introduction to the deep trouble, pal. The real deep trouble is that my sister won't believe all I collected was twenty-nine cents."

"But that *is* all you collected."

"She thinks I've got paper money—big bucks—stashed away somewhere. She keeps going, 'All right, where's the rest of it?' She even searched my room. I mean, I am actually going to have to come up with some folding money to satisfy her."

"How much?"

"Maybe as much as five dollars, and I don't have it. My allowance was cut off two months ago when my mom found those magazines under my mattress."

On the TV, Superman was trying to fight a man in a diner who had insulted him, but his powers were gone, lost at the North Pole. Jackson felt it served Superman right.

Goat cleared his throat. "Do you think your mom would be willing to cough up a buck or two for UNICEF?"

"Sure, so would I."

"Thanks. If that doesn't satisfy her, I'll have to really go out and panhandle. The trouble is, she's hidden her UNICEF stuff and I know nobody will believe I'm genuine if I don't have that. Well, I better go. My mom checks this closet every time she sees the telephone cord going under the door."

"Right. See you."

Jackson hung up the phone and tried to concentrate on Superman, only he couldn't feel sorry for him anymore. Jackson tried to imagine having those awesome powers, to be able to right wrongs, to be able to put on a red cape and fly over to Alma's and pick up Billy Ray and take him two miles up in the atmosphere and threaten to drop him if he ever hurt her again. Imagine having that kind of power and giving it up for a few moments of passion at the North Pole. Jackson clicked off the TV set in disgust.

The phone rang again and he picked it up.

"It's me again."

"Is anything else wrong, Goat?" Goat's voice had that flat, unhappy tone.

"Everything is wrong. I went in my sister's room and said, 'Rachel, you were right. The truth is that I collected three dollars.' It was a confession, Jackie. I was really humble, and you know how I hate to be humble. I went all the way. I said I hadn't told her because that was the exact amount I needed for the movie and popcorn. And she said—this is the kind of terrible person she is—she said, 'Oh, no, you collected more than that. How much did you really collect? I want every single penny of that money.' " He groaned. "Nothing is going to satisfy her— I can see that now—she's going to keep bleeding me for the rest of my life. It's like a hit man from the Mafia's after me."

"Maybe after you give her the three dollars—"

"Come on. You know Rachel better than that. After I give her the three dollars, she's going to want three more dollars, and then three more dollars. I see how people get started in a life of crime."

"What can I do?"

"Talk to her for me."

"I have not had much success in the past, pal," Jackson reminded him.

"I know, but it won't hurt to try."

"It won't work."

"Please."

"Oh, all right. Put her on."

"Rachel! Telephone!" Goat called.

While Jackson waited for Rachel to come to the phone, he started going over all the times he had tried to talk to her in the past.

"Rachel, the reason Goat and I were trying on your dresses was because we were going to be hags for Halloween and . . ."

"Rachel, Goat and I were not spying on you and David Ferguson. The reason we were behind the sofa with the tape recorder was because we were plugging it in to do a science report and you and David came in and we didn't want to disturb you and so we thought we would just hide until you were through and . . ."

"Rachel, Goat and I were not trying to read your diary. Goat and I had just seen a show on TV where a burglar opens a safe with a thumbtack and neither of us believed it could be done and so we got a thumbtack and the only small lock we could find was . . ."

"Rachel?" Jackson's voice wavered with the certainty of failure.

"Who is this?"

"It's me. Jackson."

"What do *you* want?"

The feel of failure thickened the air, made it harder to breathe.

"Rachel, I just wanted to tell you that Goat really did collect only twenty-nine cents this afternoon. The three

dollars were going to be a donation from me and my mom
and he honestly does not have any—"

Slam. Dial tone.

Another conversation with Rachel had come to an
abrupt end.

Doing Anything
Cheerfully

"Does that sound too desperate?"

Goat had just handed Jackson a small card he had printed. It read:

> We will do anything cheerfully.
> $1.00 an hour
> Jackson Hunter   Ralph McMillan

Jackson handed it back. "It does have a slightly desperate ring to it."

"Well, I feel desperate. Last night Rachel finally announced how much money she thinks I collected for

UNICEF. You know how much it is?"

"No."

"Nine dollars."

"How'd she come up with that figure?"

"I don't know, but that's what she said. Nine dollars. She wouldn't even bargain." He looked down at the card in his hand. "I thought I'd get this Xeroxed and we could pass them around the neighborhood."

"All right."

"You'll do it?"

"Yes."

"You'll help me?"

"Sure. It's my fault you're in trouble. You wouldn't have to have nine dollars if you hadn't tried to help me and Alma."

"Well, that's true, only I wasn't sure you'd see it like that I'll try to have the cards ready by tomorrow. If we can line up enough jobs for Saturday, maybe I can have a peaceful Sunday for a change."

Jackson and Goat were raking leaves Saturday morning— Mrs. Marino's yard—and it was the third yard they had raked. "Bad news, pal," Goat had said. "All the cards brought us was leaf jobs."

Mrs. Marino was watching them out the window to make sure they didn't goof off.

Every now and then she would come to the door to call, "I'm not paying you boys to jump up and down in leaf piles."

"We're tamping down them, Mrs. Marino, so we can get more in the bags."

Five minutes later: "I'm not paying you boys to put each other in leaf bags."

"It's a good way to open them up, Mrs. Marino."

They had finally filled five bags with Marino leaves when Goat stopped and put his hand to his eyes. "There she is."

"Who?"

"Alma."

Jackson spun around.

Alma was at the corner, waiting to cross the street. Nicole was on her hip. Alma always took Nicole out of the stroller when she crossed the street. She had once told Jackson, "It just worries me to death to see the way some mothers cross the street, pushing their strollers out in front of the traffic, in front of the cars, Cracker! I always carry Nicole so she'll be safe."

"I'll be right back," Jackson said. He dropped his rake and ran down the sidewalk. "Alma! Wait!"

She glanced over her shoulder, but when she saw it was Jackson, she hurried across the street, Nicole bouncing on her hip, the stroller bumping awkwardly behind her.

Jackson had to wait for some cars, so she was halfway down the next block when he caught up with her. She sighed, surrendering to his company, and put Nicole in her stroller.

"Why were you running from me?" he asked.

"I was running because I was in a wreck last week and

I knew as soon as you saw me you'd start in about Billy Ray hitting me. I didn't want to see you until I looked normal."

She had put on some makeup to hide the bruises, but it somehow made them look worse to Jackson. He said, "No, I didn't think that. If you tell me you've been in a wreck, I believe you've been in a wreck."

"Really?"

"Yes."

She smiled then, the first smile he had seen on her face in a long time. "All right, then. That's the bad news. I was in a wreck. Now for the good."

"What's that?"

"Nicole has a tooth! Her first tooth! Want to see?"

"Sure."

"Wait till I open her mouth."

Alma bent by the stroller. "Cupcake, Cracker wants to see your tooth. Now, you'll have to look real close, Cracker, because it's just barely through the gum. Nobody but me can see it. There."

Jackson knelt on the sidewalk and looked closely at the pink gum.

"See it?"

"I think so."

"Here, give me your finger. I'll let you feel it."

"No, my hands are dirty. I've been raking leaves. I—"

But before he could stop her, she had pressed his finger

to Nicole's gum and he felt the tiny ridge of her first tooth.

"Did you feel it?"

"Yes."

"Really? Or are you just saying that to make me happy?"

"I really felt it."

"I knew you would, Cracker. I can always count on you." Alma straightened. "Well, I've got to go. I'm going over to Mary's. Her baby's having a party. Freddie's two months old today. Nicole's taking him a little rubber duck, aren't you, Sweet Pea?"

Jackson fell into step beside them.

"This is Nicole's first party. I'm going to paste the funny hat in her scrapbook—I know we're having funny hats because Mary told me. Well, here we are. You be sweet, Cracker."

"I will."

"Bye."

Jackson stood in the middle of the sidewalk and watched as they went up the steps. Alma got Nicole out of the stroller, turned, waved one of Nicole's hands in his direction, and rang the bell.

When Jackson got back to the Marino yard, Goat was nowhere in sight. He called, "Goat, I'm back." When there was no answer, he started for the house. Maybe a miracle had happened and Mrs. Marino had invited Goat in for a Coke.

Suddenly he heard leaves rustling behind him. He turned, and the pile of leaves was stirring, and strange noises—

growls—were coming from it. Goat rose up, arms out-stretched, monster-style.

This was a game they had played the first fall of their friendship—Leaf Monster. Jackson prepared to make the expected tackle. Arms outstretched, he—

"Boys!" It was Mrs. Marino again. "I'm not paying you to play in the leaves."

"We were playing that time, Mrs. Marino," Goat admitted. He began to brush the leaves from his sweater in a businesslike manner. "It was just a brief moment of frivolity, however. You can deduct it from our wages." He turned to Jackson. "How is she?"

"Better," he answered. He hoped with all his heart it was true.

Sister Rose

"I saw Alma in the store today."

The book Jackson was reading dropped to the floor. It had been ten days since he had seen Alma going to Freddie's birthday party.

And in those ten days, Goat had gone to her house twice. He had printed a little card that said "Thank you for supporting UNICEF," which he was going to give to her. Both times she would not come to the door. Jackson himself had telephoned twice to ask if Nicole had had a good time at the party, but both times Billy Ray answered, and he had to hang up.

"How was she?"

"She was fine," his mother said. "She had Nicole with her and they were shopping for an outfit for Nicole to have her picture made in. In case you are interested, Nicole will be photographed in a red organdy dress with a white pinafore and red ribbons in her hair. Alma wants to make little pigtails, but she doesn't think Nicole's hair will be long enough by Friday."

His mother went into the kitchen to put up the groceries. He tagged along.

"And did she really look all right?"

"She looked fine. She seemed very happy." His mom started putting the groceries away as if this were ordinary information instead of headline, world-shaking news.

"Alma said Billy Ray had given her twenty dollars to go shopping," she went on. "She and Nicole love to go shopping."

"Anything else?" He was thirsty for the smallest detail about her well-being.

"Let's see. She said if she had any money left over after buying the red organdy dress, she was going to buy Nicole a jogging suit she had seen at Sky City."

"I can't believe it."

Jackson sank down at the table. He was weak with relief. For the past ten days his imagination had been running wild. He had thought she might have been hurt too badly to come to the door. He had even thought she might be dead.

"She also said that if the pictures turn out, she will send

us one. She says she can have the little pictures made into heart-shaped lockets that look like real gold, but I said a plain photograph would be fine."

"And she really looked all right?"

"How many times do I have to tell you? Honestly, Jackson, from the way you've been carrying on, I fully expected to see her in a body cast. Alma looked as happy as I have ever seen her. She was positively radiant."

That last remark satisfied Jackson. He had seen Alma like that one time—radiant—and so he knew what his mother meant. When Alma was really happy, she shone, actually glowed. It was something nobody could put on. He went back to his homework happy.

One summer when Alma was baby-sitting for him, she took him across town on the bus. This was their longest trip—they had to transfer twice—because Alma needed to have her palm read by a woman named Sister Rose. Alma said Sister Rose could tell you everything that would happen to you in your whole life. Sister Rose was never wrong. She had told Alma's cousin that she was going to have twins, a boy and a girl, and even the doctor hadn't believed it until they both popped out.

Jackson didn't care about things like that, but he enjoyed the bus rides. It wasn't just the pleasure of doing something his mother wouldn't approve of, it was that the destinations were always places of interest—the garage, a secondhand shop, a friend's beauty parlor where the beauticians made him a mustache out of somebody's cut-off hair. "Groucho Marx!" everyone cried when he was turned around in the chair. He had wanted to keep that mustache on forever.

"The reason I want to have my palm read," Alma told him on the bus, "is because I want to know if Billy Ray and I are going to get married. Do you think we'll get married?"

"Yes."

She gave him the kiss on the forehead that always followed a right answer. "Oh, I love you, Cupcake. You always say the right thing." Then she went back to looking serious. "I hope so, but I don't know. My mom says I'm chasing him, that I shouldn't go over to the garage so much, but I like to go over there—don't you?"

"Yes."

Another kiss on the forehead. Then she opened her hand—she wore rings on all her fingers—and looked carefully at the lines in her palm. "I'll just die if she tells me we won't get married. I'll just die."

"Me, too."

At this sympathetic and heart-felt statement, she put her arm around Jackson and hugged him so hard his shoulders touched his ears.

"Oh, I love you, Cracker. I just don't know what I'd do if I didn't have you to talk to."

At Sister Rose's he waited out in the living room on the sofa while Alma went in to have her palm read. The room was dark and there were lots of cats prowling around. The cats never came out in the open where Jackson could see them, just slunk around behind the furniture.

Jackson was never able to get an exact head count, but he knew there were an awful lot of cats in there. He could catch glimpses of white fur, yellow fur, the gleam of golden eyes set in black fur. He would not have sat any quieter if he had been surrounded by lions.

The shades were drawn, the windows shut, the air smelling of cats—a smell Jackson had never smelled before but would never forget—and when Alma came out he was sitting in the exact same place she had left him, with his hands folded in his lap.

Alma swept him up into her arms and began to dance wildly around the cluttered room.

He and Alma danced a lot at home when his mother wasn't there. Alma was a good dancer and they slow-danced and frugged and even tangoed, with Jackson's feet never touching the floor. His favorite was the clog. But never before had they danced with such abandon. He grew dizzy with pleasure.

"Oh, Cracker," she said. She kissed him. Around them the cats seemed to be whirling, too. The whole world had turned into a giant merry-go-round of happiness.

"Yes, Cracker, yes. I'm going to marry him!"

And, in the dim light of Sister Rose's living room, her face shone with enough glow to brighten the whole room. He had not known it was possible for a person to be that happy. He never had been. His mother never had been. Not even his carefree father.

Jackson felt he had been let in on one of the best-kept

secrets of the adult world—total, complete happiness. For the first time in his life, he was willing to be big.

Sister Rose appeared in the doorway. She was a short, stocky woman in a chenille bathrobe. She shook her frizzy head sadly. "But, my dear, you will live to regret it," she said.

"Never," Alma said. She threw back her head and laughed at the impossibility. "Never in a million, trillion years."

She kissed Jackson again and they waltzed out the door.

The Double Hurt

"Cracker?"

The voice on the phone quivered. It was an old voice. It could not possibly be Alma's, and yet nobody else ever called him Cracker.

"Alma? Is this you?"

"Yes."

"What's happened? Are you all right?"

"No."

The voice was hers, and yet not hers. It was like her voice would sound when she was ninety years old and life wasn't good anymore.

"What's wrong?"

"Billy Ray."

The name and the way she said it turned him cold. He shivered in the overheated living room. "He hurt you." It was a statement, not a question.

Silence.

"Alma, did he hurt you?"

"It wasn't me he hurt."

"Who, then?"

Silence.

"Alma, who? Tell me."

"Nicole."

The phone was suddenly so heavy, his arms so weak, that he fumbled the receiver. He said, "Oh, Alma."

He was overcome with sadness, a kind of sadness he had not known even when his dad left for L.A. This was the kind of sadness, he realized, that comes when the whole world goes wrong, when it grinds down like a broken machine, and you know that even if it does get started again, it will never work quite the same again.

"I don't know what I'm going to do, Cracker."

"Can't you tell your mom?" He tried to remember Alma's mother. He had met her several times—Alma had taken him to her house a lot—but in his mind her features were dimmed by a cloud of cigarette smoke.

"I don't even know where Mama is. Didn't I tell you? She went off to Kansas City with her boyfriend six months ago."

"No."

"She didn't even leave an address."

"Oh."

"I don't know what I'm going to do, Cracker. I just don't know what I'm going to do. I don't mind if he hits me—I told him so. I said, 'Billy Ray, just hit me all you want to, only leave Nicole alone.' "

"He hit Nicole?" Jackson asked again. He had read in the paper and heard on the news about people hurting little children, but he had not really believed it.

"I was supposed to take her to have her picture made. I had got her a new outfit and ribbons to put in her hair and Billy Ray came in and I never saw him so mad. He had fixed this man's car and he had it running perfectly and the bank called and said the man had stopped payment on the check. The man said the car never made it home. He said the engine died in the fast lane of I-85. Billy Ray had a hundred and forty-six dollars in parts in that man's car. That's a hundred and forty-six dollars out of Billy Ray's pocket."

"I know."

"Billy Ray came in the house and I was getting Nicole dressed and he said, 'Can't you leave that kid alone for five minutes?' I said, 'Billy Ray, this is the day she gets her picture made. Remember, you said she could?' He said, 'Well, now I say she can't.' I said, 'Billy Ray, please, I want these pictures real bad. Nicole's never had a real picture taken.' I said, 'I'll do anything if you just let me take her to Sky City and be photographed by a real photographer.' He said, 'No.' I started to say, 'Please,' again, and before I got the word out, he reached out and hit me. He hit me hard, Cracker. I lied to you before. He does hit me, and this time he hit me so hard, I fell down on the floor. It scared me because it was the first time he ever hit me when I was holding the baby.''

"Is that how he hurt her?"

"No, it gets worse, Cracker."

"Oh."

"I got up, and I was holding my hand over Nicole's head for protection. I said, 'Let me put the baby in her crib.' Billy Ray said, 'I'll put the baby in her crib,' and he yanked Nicole out of my arms and went in and just threw her in her crib. I tried to stop him, but he pushed me down and I couldn't get up fast enough. Nicole was crying her heart out—nobody had ever done her like that before—and, Cracker, it just tore me to pieces to hear her cry like that."

Jackson could not answer.

"Billy Ray was like a crazy man. He said, 'Shut up!'— this was to Nicole. He was leaning over the crib. I was crawling over there as fast as I could. 'Shut up!' he said again. Then he hit her."

It was too much. Jackson couldn't breathe. It was like all the oxygen had suddenly been drained from the room. He said, "Alma, you've got to get out of there. He's going to kill both of you."

"I don't have anywhere to go, Cracker. One time I went to my girlfriend's and he came over there and dragged me home and beat me worse. That's how I got that black eye. He'll find me no matter where I go."

"You could call the police."

"The police don't care."

"They do. They have to. It's their job."

"He'd come over to the police station—I know him, Cracker—and he'd act so sorry and he'd promise never to do it again and the police would believe him. His first cousin is a highway patrolman. I don't know what I'm going to do. I don't mind him hitting me, but I just can't stand it, Cracker, when he's mean to Nicole."

"I can't stand it when he's mean to either one of you."

"Is your mama there, Cracker? Maybe she could help me."

"She's in Chicago. My sitter's supposed to get here at seven, but I don't think she could help. Where is Billy Ray right now?"

"He went off. I don't know where he is. Usually when he beats me up, he goes off for a while, and then when he comes back, he's better."

"Wait a minute," he said. "Mom said something about a place women can go if their husbands beat them. I think she said it's in Avondale. Why don't you go there?"

"I don't have any way to get there."

"How about your girlfriend?"

"She might drive me, but she'd tell Billy Ray. He would go over there first thing. Everybody's afraid of him, Cracker. There's not anybody who wouldn't tell him where I went if he leaned on them. I just don't have any friends strong enough to lie to Billy Ray. I don't blame them. I'm scared of him, too. I—"

"I'll drive you," he said.

"What?"

"I'll drive you."

"Cracker, you can't drive."

"Yes, I can. My mom's been letting me pull into the driveway ever since school started."

"Pulling into the driveway is not going to Avondale."

"I can do it, I tell you, and I've got a friend who'll help me."

"Does he have a driver's license?"

"Not yet, but he can drive. He has a lot of driving experience."

"Who is your friend, Cracker? Would he be willing to go? Would he tell Billy Ray? What's his name?"

Jackson swallowed hard, gulping down air, so he could bring up the name of his friend.

"Goat," he said.

A
Two-Pillow
Drive

"Goat?"

"Yes, it's me. What time is it?"

Jackson looked at the clock. "Seven-thirty."

"Don't you know it's Saturday? Don't you know—"

"Goat," he interrupted, "we have to drive to Avondale."

"What?"

"You heard right. We have to drive to Avondale."

"You got to be kidding."

"No."

"Jackson"—this was the first time Jackson had ever heard Goat use his real name—"we cannot drive to Avondale."

"Yes, we can."

"You do remember, don't you, what happened the last time I drove? I was just going to help my mom out by pulling the car into the garage—a little surprise. My foot slipped and I went through the garage and into the laundry room and totaled the washer-dryer."

"That could have happened to anybody."

"Not according to my mom."

Actually this was the driving experience Jackson had had in mind when he told Alma his friend had experience. That and this: When Goat was little, his grandfather would let him sit on his lap and steer his Oldsmobile. They used to drive all over town like that, the grandfather pressing the gas, Goat steering.

Then one day Goat's mother saw them. She was coming out of the Piggly Wiggly, and Goat and his grandfather were attempting a U-turn in the middle of Main Street. The grandfather was saying "Wheeeeee!" Goat's mom dropped her groceries, she was so horrified to see Goat at the wheel.

Later, after he had been forbidden to let Goat steer again, the grandfather started letting their dog, a Boston bull, take Goat's place. The Boston bull—Pug was his name—couldn't really drive, of course, but the grandfather would hold his paws on the wheel so that it looked as if Pug were really steering.

Goat's mother found out about this because Pug was no longer satisfied to ride on the seat of the family car.

He was always trying to climb onto the driver's lap so he could steer. Goat's mother kept saying, "What is wrong with this crazy dog?" and Goat, who was jealous that Pug got to steer in his place, one day blurted out the truth: "Paw-Paw lets Pug drive." After that, nobody in the family was allowed to ride in Paw-Paw's Oldsmobile.

"You have forgotten one important thing," Goat said now, "we do not have wheels."

When Goat said that, Jackson knew the matter was settled. When Goat started thinking up reasons why they couldn't do something, it was because he really wanted to.

"I can get my mom's car."

"She takes it to the airport."

"Not the Cutlass. She takes the Omni because she doesn't care if it gets dented in the parking lot."

"You're taking the Cutlass Supreme?" Goat's voice rose with astonishment. Jackson's mom was very particular about the Cutlass. One time she drove them home from Scouts and made them sit on plastic bags so they wouldn't get the seats messy.

"Yes."

"Why don't we wait for the Omni? If we wreck the Omni, it won't be so bad. We—"

"I can't wait for the Omni! We've got to go today!"

"All right, I'll take your word for it. Only why does it have to be Avondale? Why don't we just tool around town. I'd go for that."

"Goat, we have to take Alma to Avondale. There's this place over there where you can go if your husband beats you, and yesterday Billy Ray beat her and he hit the baby." His voice broke with the pain of putting this terrible thing into words."

"Oh. Okay. Avondale it is." Goat sighed. "I don't even know where Avondale is. I've never even been to Avondale."

"There are maps in the car."

"Have you ever had a good look at a map, pal? It's just a bunch of lines. It doesn't tell you a thing."

"I'll get us out of town. I promise. I've been to Avondale a hundred times. My uncle lives in Avondale."

There was a silence while Goat thought about it. Jackson could almost hear the whirr of his brain evaluating all the information. "We'll need pillows. If any cop sees how little we are, he'll pull us over."

"I'll get pillows."

"We'll have to take back roads."

"We will."

"We can't stop for gas. No gas attendant will sell us gas if we're underage."

"My mom keeps the tank full."

"Okay, but I get to do half of the driving."

"It's a deal."

Jackson was going down the steps with the pillows when he met Kim, his Saturday baby-sitter, coming up. Kim lived in the apartment across the hall and kept an eye on him during the day when his mother was late getting back from a trip.

"You going out?" Kim asked.

"I have to return these pillows."

"You must have had some company."

"Yes," he lied. He paused on the landing. "After I return the pillows, I'm going over to my friend's house. Mom says it's all right."

"Okay. Check with me later."

"I will." Again he paused. "Oh, Kim . . .

"What?"

"Which way is Avondale?"

"Avondale . . . Avondale . . . I think it's out past the drive-in."

"Thanks."

He ran out the door and into the apartment building's garage. He was relieved to see that it was empty. With hands that trembled, he unlocked the Cutlass's door, slid the seat forward and sat on the pillow. He put the key in the ignition.

He sat there for a moment, breathing quietly. His nose had started to run. He wiped it on his sleeve.

He used to hope somebody would invent a Kleenex that would clamp over your nose. He dreamed once he saw such a commercial on TV. "For that eternally running nose, here's Pinchex, the tissue that clamps on your nose, keeps your upper lip dry, and leaves your hands free for brain surgery."

Dear Pinchex, he had written in his dream, *please send*

me a truckload of your fine product immediately. . . .

He turned the key and the engine roared instantly into life. He shifted the gear to reverse, pressed the gas pedal, and the Cutlass shot out of the parking slot like a comet. He braked so hard his head rammed into the steering wheel. He tasted blood.

He took a few breaths to calm himself. He had not known how quickly a car could respond. The Cutlass was acting like a horse eager to be out of the barn.

The deep breaths weren't helping, so he shifted the gear to forward and turned the wheel a quarter turn—that should be more than enough. It was. The Cutlass turned in such a tight circle that he had to go around in another tight circle the other way to get out of the garage.

He turned onto the street and noticed for the first time how narrow it was. And the Cutlass was as wide as a six-wheeler. He would never be able to squeeze it through this tiny lane.

He cowered as a car passed, going in the other direction. He waited for the crunch of metal.

Well, he thought, when the crunch didn't come, I guess I'm on my way. Very slowly, he stepped on the gas.

On the Road

Goat was waiting on the corner. They had arranged this because if either his mother or Rachel saw Jackson pulling up in front of the house, the trip to Avondale would, as Goat put it, "come to a screeching halt."

As soon as Goat saw Jackson, his face lit up. He put out his thumb like a hitchhiker.

Jackson would have given a lot to stop right next to him, but he had not caught on to the brakes yet. He stopped three times—once twenty feet away, once ten feet away, and in a last effort, he went up on the curb and almost hit a tree.

Goat got in eagerly. There was an air of festivity as he

settled himself on his pillow and buckled his seat belt. "No offense, pal," he said, "but you better buckle up, too. We are not in the hands of an experienced driver."

Jackson pressed the gas pedal and they shot forward, off the curb and onto the street.

"Stop sign ahead," Goat said.

"I see it."

Jackson was tense. He had not realized how much there was to driving. His parents always made it look easy. Most of the time his father used only one hand.

"You know where the brakes are, don't you?" Goat asked.

"Yes."

"Where?"

"I've already used them three times, Goat." He groped on the floor for the pedal.

"Better make it four pretty quick because this stop sign is—"

Jackson slammed on the brakes, and both boys lunged forward.

"—coming up fast," Goat finished.

Once again, Jackson had stopped short of his goal. "Look, pal," Goat said, "with these power brakes, you just barely press down, all right? You want me to drive?"

"No!"

"Now, wait a minute. Wait a minute. You said I could drive. You promised."

"You can drive, but not now!"

"All right." Goat settled back in his seat. "So, where are we picking up Alma?"

"She's meeting us behind the grocery store. She doesn't want anybody to see her getting in the car because she doesn't want Billy Ray to know."

"Me either. I mean, what if he found out and started chasing us? We are not ready for one of those *Dukes of Hazzard* car chases, pal. You better get ready to turn. The grocery store's coming up."

"I see it."

Jackson had been driving only five minutes, but already his body ached. His shoulders were hunched up to his ears and his hands were clutching the steering wheel so tightly they would have to be pried off. He had a cramp in his gas-pedal foot.

"Easy does it," Goat said.

"Right."

In a wide arc, Jackson turned into the parking lot, using both lanes. He missed a Chevy and a Ford station wagon, and swung to the back of the store.

"Nice going," Goat said. "I couldn't have done better myself. Oh, there she is."

Alma was standing by the garbage dumpster, with Nicole on her hip. Slung over her shoulder was a large blue diaper bag. She came forward anxiously as soon as she saw them.

In one easy movement, Goat undid his seat belt and

leaned over to open the rear door. "There you go!" he
said gallantly.

"I've been so worried you weren't going to come."

"You knew I would," Jackson said.

"Cracker, I knew you would if you possibly could, but
I just can't count on anything anymore."

She slid into the back seat. She said, "If Billy Ray knew
we were doing this, he'd kill us."

"Maybe you better get down on the floor," Goat sug-
gested quickly.

"All right."

"Just until we get out of town."

Alma dropped down onto the floor of the back seat. "I
didn't think I was going to get out of the house. Billy Ray
came home right after I talked to you, and he wouldn't
let me out of his sight. I said I just had to run to the store
for five minutes. I didn't dare bring anything with me but
the diaper bag. I had to leave all of my clothes, all of my
Barbies, all of Nicole's little outfits."

Goat leaned forward against his seat belt to peer around
the grocery store. "Coast is clear," he announced.

Jackson pulled around the store and into the parking
lot. He suddenly remembered the first time Alma had
taken him to her house. It had been to show him her
Barbie collection. He had been awed by the chorus line
of unplayed-with dolls. "This is Malibu Barbie, this is
Tiffany, this is Crystal Barbie . . ." He'd gaped at the ski
outfits, the bikinis, the tiny sunglasses, the rows of min-

iature high heels. "And I never play with them," she'd told him unnecessarily. "When I have a little girl I want her to have every Barbie ever made."

"She will," he'd said.

"You might as well let these two cars get out of the way," Goat advised. "There are a lot of poor drivers on the roads these days. Okay. Now go."

As if on command, Jackson drove through the parking lot and onto the road and turned right. "This is the way to the drive-in, isn't it?" he asked through his teeth. His jaws were clenched so tightly he wondered if he would ever speak normally again.

"Man, you said you knew where Avondale was. You said you'd been there hundreds of times."

"I know. I have. I just wanted to make sure."

In the back seat Nicole began to cry. Jackson had not thought it was possible to get any more nervous than he already was, but now he saw that a person could keep on getting more and more nervous until eventually . . . Suddenly the term "nervous breakdown" took on real meaning.

"Is anything wrong back there?" he asked through his teeth.

"No." Alma shifted Nicole to her shoulder to muffle her crying. "It's just so sad. I mean, Nicole knows something's wrong, don't you, Pumpkin? I wish I could get her pacifier out of the diaper bag."

"Get the pacifier, Goat," Jackson said.

"Right."

Goat rummaged through Pampers and bottles and baby clothes until he found the pacifier. Nicole was screaming now.

"Poor little thing. She doesn't know why she has to be on the floor of the car, do you, Angel? You don't know what's happened. Your whole life's changed, and— Oh, thanks." She put the pacifier in Nicole's mouth, and a wonderful silence filled the car.

"Stoplight coming up," Goat warned. "You might be able to slip through on the yellow, but maybe you better get ready to stop. Don't stop so far back this time. I read somewhere that the police arrest people who stop too far back, because that's what drunks do. They want to be so sure they stop that they stop way, way back, like you just—"

Jackson made another of his abrupt stops.

"Don't do that!" Goat said. "You're giving me whiplash injuries."

"I'm sorry!"

When the light changed, Jackson eased across the intersection.

"Well, that's good news," Goat said. "Did you see that sign, pal?"

"No, I was watching the road."

"Good idea. The sign said 'Avondale.' We're going in the right direction."

"How many miles?"

"Twenty-six."

Goat's cheerful voice made twenty-six miles sound like the ideal distance for a Saturday jaunt. To Jackson, twenty-six miles was the same as a thousand.

"Would it disturb anybody if I turned on the radio?" Goat leaned over the back seat. "Would the baby mind?"

"Nicole loves music—don't you, Doughnut."

"Rock or country?"

"She likes all kinds."

Jackson took his eyes from the road for a second to check the speedometer. Above all things, he did not want to get pulled over for speeding. They were doing a brisk twenty-six miles an hour.

At this rate, with a lot of luck, they would get to Avondale in exactly one hour. In his mind he repeated the key phrase: with a lot of luck.

Almost to Avondale

They had gone fifteen miles before Alma felt safe enough to get up off the floor of the back seat. The first thing she did was look out the rear window to see if they were being followed. When she saw that the road was clear, she leaned against the seat and sighed.

"I know he's looking for me."

"Maybe not," Goat said. He did not even glance at Alma. For the last fourteen miles Goat had been begging Jackson to let him drive. "Well, when am I going to get a turn?" he asked. "I know what you're going to do. You're going to wait until we're almost there and then you'll let me drive the last ten feet like my dad. I want to drive out here, where I can build up a little speed."

"I'll stop in a minute."

"You've been saying that for an hour."

"It wouldn't be like Billy Ray not to come looking for me," Alma went on, having a conversation with herself. She glanced over her shoulder, out the back window again. "That's probably what he's doing right now. If either of you see a blue pickup truck, let me know so I can get down."

"Are you going to let me drive home—yes or no?"

"I guess so." The memory of Goat's assault on the laundry room had been getting more and more vivid in Jackson's mind, making him less and less eager to turn over the wheel to him.

"You guess so? Well, you better or I'm not ever driving anywhere with you again."

"All right!"

"Billy Ray's probably over at Margie's—Margie's my girlfriend. She just lives about a block from the store, and he'll figure I stopped in for a Coke. But I won't be there and then he'll go to his mom's and I won't be there, either— Oh, what if he thinks I've been kidnapped? What if he calls the police?"

"It's unlikely he'd call the police," Goat said, turning to peer at her around his headrest. "Not considering what he's done."

"He never means to hit me," Alma said. "It's like something builds up in him. You know the first time he hit me?

It was because the Falcons lost a football game. He'd been sitting there drinking beer all evening, cheering them on, and when they lost, well, he couldn't stand it and he hit me. He probably doesn't even think he's doing anything wrong."

"He knows he's doing something wrong," Goat said.

"He didn't used to be like that, did he, Cracker? Remember when we used to go to the garage? He was so sweet to you. You weren't even tall enough to see under the hood, and he'd hold you up and let you check the oil. 'I need somebody to help me check this oil,' he'd say, and you'd just come running and jump up in his arms."

There was a long pause. Alma said, "He can still be sweet like that when he wants to. You're going to miss your daddy, aren't you, Muffin?"

Then there was an even longer pause. It was such a long pause that it seemed to Jackson that it grew, it developed, the way a stream you can step across at one place becomes a creek, a river, a sea.

Then Alma put the huge, unspeakable thought into words. "Maybe we ought to turn around."

"What?" Goat said. "*What?*"

Jackson could not speak. Like a robot, he kept driving down the road, hunched over the steering wheel.

Alma said it again. "Maybe we ought to turn around."

"I cannot believe I'm hearing this," Goat said.

Jackson still could not speak.

"What do you think, Cracker?"

He managed to say, "I think we ought to keep going."

"I just wonder what everybody will think, that's all," Alma said.

"They'll think you got smart," Goat said.

"His mama probably won't ever speak to me again. She doesn't see anything wrong with Billy Ray hitting me. She told me one time that Billy Ray's dad used to beat up on her all the time until his arthritis got bad. What do you think, Cracker?"

"He told you what he thought. Keep driving."

"Pull over, Cracker, please. I need to think."

"Keep driving," Goat said.

"Please, Cracker, just give me a minute. I can't think while we're speeding along. Please!"

It was hard for Jackson to deny Alma anything when she got that desperate sound in her voice. He pulled off the road and stopped the car. He rested his forehead against the steering wheel.

As he hung there, exhausted, he remembered how, when they used to go on vacation, his dad would drive three or four hours at a stretch. He had only been driving—he opened one eye to check his watch—twenty minutes, and he was ready for bed. Suddenly he wanted his father in that old, lump-in-the-throat way he had wanted him when he first went away.

Goat turned down the radio. The sudden silence in the car made the moment more tense.

Alma said absently, "Don't put your fingers in my

mouth, Patty Cake. Mama's trying to think."

Goat began to drum his fingers against his armrest.

Then Alma's voice burst with desperation. "I just wish somebody would tell me what to do!"

Goat said, "Alma, that's what we're doing. Jackie and I think you better get away from your husband before you and the baby get killed." He said it in such a serious, adult voice that it made instant sense. Jackson glanced at his friend with appreciation. Alma had to be impressed, too.

"I want to go home," she said suddenly, in a new, firm voice.

"No, Alma, listen," Jackson said. "It's not just you. It's Nicole he's going to hurt. You don't want Nicole to be hurt. That's the whole point. You—"

"I want to go home."

"Alma—"

"I mean it. I want to go home. If you won't take me, I'll walk."

"Alma!"

She started cramming stuff in the diaper bag. She buttoned Nicole's sweater. She slung the diaper bag over her shoulder. She put her hand on the door.

"I'll take you," Jackson said. He had never felt so tired, so defeated in his whole life. His nose started running like a faucet. His mom had a special holder for tissues in the Cutlass and he took some and pinched his nose shut.

"I'll drive," Goat said quickly.

"I'd appreciate it."

Goat and Jackson got out and passed each other in front of the car. Goat was so happy to be taking the wheel that he grabbed Jackson's arm and swung him around in a do-si-do square-dance step.

Jackson came out of the turn like a hundred-year-old man. He struggled to the car and took the shotgun seat. He lay back and closed his eyes.

Beside him Goat began to whistle "On the Road Again." He broke off to say, "Everybody buckled up?" and checked their seat belts as closely as Jackson's mother checked her Eastern passengers'. "Then here goes." He stepped on the gas.

The car wheels spun in the dirt beside the road and then caught. The car swerved in a tight circle back onto the road and into—at least Jackson had this to be grateful for—the right lane.

"In the back seat Alma said, "Cracker?"

"What?"

"You aren't mad at me, are you?"

"No."

"I couldn't stand it if you were mad at me. It would just be too much on top of everything else."

Jackson looked back, and her eyes were filled with tears. Her eyes could hold more tears than anybody's he ever saw.

"I'm not mad," he said.

Home Again, Home Again, Riggidy-Jig

"Oh, hi, Jackson, I was just coming over to see if I could fix you something to eat." It was Kim. Jackson was coming up the stairs, one step at a time, like a tired child. He had a pillow under each arm.

"I'm not very hungry."

This, Jackson felt, was the understatement of the year. Goat's final swing down Oak Street had taken away his appetite for the rest of his natural life.

"There's Percy Gill!" Goat had cried. He had changed lanes instantly. Brakes squealed behind them. "Hey, Perce!" Goat sounded the horn, a long blast followed by two short ones. He fumbled for the window control. "How do you get these windows down?"

"Watch what you're doing!" Jackson was on the edge of his seat, straining against his seat belt. "Goat—"

"Hey, Perce, look at me. I'm driving!"

And in the exhilaration of being spotted by Percy Gill, Goat went through a red light at the intersection.

The next few seconds were like something out of a TV car chase. They missed a mail truck by two feet, a station wagon by two inches, and a Ford sedan by a miracle. More horns were blown than on New Year's Eve.

"Close one," Goat said.

In the back seat Nicole spit out her pacifier and burst into tears. In the front seat, Jackson felt like joining her.

Kim watched Jackson's slow progress up the stairs. "Are you all right?"

"I'm fine. I'll get something to eat later."

"Did you have a good time at your friend's house?"

"Not really."

Jackson unlocked the apartment door and went inside. He sank down on the sofa, the pillows on his lap.

As he sat there, he tried to tell himself all the many things he had to be grateful for. One, he had not wrecked the car. Two—more surprising—Goat had not wrecked the car. Three, Goat had managed to park in the exact spot his mom had been in. Four, he had remembered to put the driver's seat back and to remove the used tissues.

None of this mattered. All that mattered was the way Alma's face had looked as they let her out at the grocery store dumpster.

"Oh, I just hope Billy Ray hasn't missed me," she had said. Her face looked pale. There were lines between her eyebrows Jackson had not noticed before. "I just hope he's been busy in the garage or somewhere and won't have noticed the time. I'm going to say I stopped in at Margie's—how does that sound? Only, he might have checked with Margie, and the worst thing you can do is lie to Billy Ray. He can't stand being lied to. Well, I'll think of something."

All this time she was getting out of the car, shifting Nicole to a more comfortable spot on her hip, adjusting the diaper bag on her shoulder.

Then she leaned back into the car. Her long, curly hair swung around her face. She touched Jackson's shoulder so lightly he didn't even feel it.

"I really appreciate what you did, Cracker," she said. "You'll always be special to me, you know that. I don't know a single other person who would have stolen his mother's car to help me get to Avondale."

There was a pause, then: "Good-bye, Cracker." She slammed the door and disappeared around the dumpster.

Goat said, "I think I'll try reverse. I've never had an occasion to— Ah, there we go. I'm getting good at this. Now forward."

He steered around the grocery store. "I do wish she

hadn't put it like that—stolen your mother's car. It makes us sound bad. 'Borrowed' is a much nicer term."

He stopped at the stop sign and then pulled onto the street. "I wish my mom could have seen that. My mom thinks I have no respect for signs." He paused at the yield sign and then turned the corner. "Can you believe the way I'm driving? All I needed was a chance. The laundry room disaster was obviously a fluke.

"The unfortunate thing," he went on, "is that I won't be able to tell my mom how well I did, because then she would want to know every detail—whose car it was, if we had permission . . . blah . . . blah . . ." He put on the brakes. "Here we are. Your apartment, sir."

"My mom always parks in this slot."

Goat pulled into the correct parking slot. "A little crooked," he said, eyeing his position. "I better straighten up. Your mom would never go over the yellow line." He backed up. "I'm beginning to enjoy this. Now, forward. If I do say so myself, that is perfect parking. Or do you think I am a titch too close on—"

"It's fine."

"It wouldn't hurt to be a titch closer—"

"It's fine!"

"All right, all right." Goat turned off the key, pulled on the parking brake . He leaned back. "Well," he said, "that is what I call a successful drive."

"It wasn't successful, Goat. We didn't get Alma to Avondale."

"Well, yeah, that part wasn't successful, but the rest, pal, you got to admit was perfect."

And as Goat got out of the car, he laid his hand on the silver fender, the way a horseman lays his hand on the flank of a horse who's given good service.

Jackson was still sitting on the sofa, cradling the pillows in his lap, when the phone rang.

He was almost too tired to answer. It was a real effort to reach for the phone. "Hello?"

"It's me, Cracker."

He found the strength to sit up.

"I just wanted you to know everything's fine. Billy Ray didn't even know I was gone. He was over at his mom's and I got home before he did." She spoke in a rush of words, her voice low. "I'll be seeing you, Cracker."

"Alma—"

"Thanks for everything."

And she was gone.

The Hanging-Up Blues

"If I didn't know better, I would swear that somebody had been driving my car."

Jackson's fork clattered to his plate. "What makes you think that, Mom?"

"There's mud on the floor."

"Probably from my shoes."

"No, this is on the driver's side."

"Oh."

"And I'm always so careful about—" The phone rang and his mother broke off to say, "I hope that is not Goat again. Why is he calling so much?"

"I don't know."

Jackson got up from the table. The reason Goat had been calling so much was to ask if Jackson could get his mom's car to drive to the movies, to the bowling alley, to the skating rink, to Percy Gill's house, or just for "a quick turn around the block, then, for old times' sake?"

This time it was Jackson's father. Jackson knew it as soon as he picked up the phone and heard an English voice say, "Sir, will you accept a collect call from the Queen of England?"

"Yes."

"Go ahead, Your Majesty." Then a falsetto voice said, "Queen Elizabeth here."

Suddenly Jackson didn't want to play anymore. For the first time in his life he understood why his mom had got tired of all the impersonations, why she used to beg, "Will you just be serious for five minutes?" There are times you don't want to talk to the Queen of England or the President of the United States. You just want your father.

He said, "Dad."

"How'd you know it was me?"

Jackson wasn't even up to the usual "I already talked to the Queen once today."

In the week since he and Goat had tried to drive Alma to Avondale, Jackson had not felt like himself. He had discovered that there is something about a failed heroic act—that's how he saw taking his mom's car to drive Alma to Avondale—there is something about a failed heroic act that turns the person himself into a failure. He might as well have put a sign on his back—failure—because no matter what he did now, no matter how hard he tried, he knew he would not succeed.

"I knew," he said in his new, hopeless voice.

"So, how are things going?"

"Oh, all right."

Jackson knew there was no point in telling his father about Alma and Nicole and Billy Ray and the failed heroic act. His father was a thousand miles away. He really might as well have been talking to the Queen.

"How's school?"

"Oh, all right."

"How's your mom? Oh, all right. How's the weather? Oh, all right. How's the situation in Kalamazoo? Oh, all right."

Now his father was imitating Jackson's voice. Suddenly it was unbearable to hear his own voice, brimming with pain, being mocked. And he could think of only one way to stop it. Jackson hung up the phone.

He stared at the silenced phone with a sort of dull surprise. He had never hung up on his father before. It was the first time he ever hung up on anybody. What he had done, he realized then, was hang up on himself.

His mother came into the room. "Was that your father?"

"Yes."

"Well, that was a short conversation."

"I know."

The phone started ringing again. "You answer it," Jack-

son said. He got up, went into his room, and shut the
door. He had once bought a "Private—Keep Out" sign
for his door, but every time he put it up, his mother came
into the room to see what was wrong.

In approximately one minute flat, the door to his room
opened and his mom came in. Jackson was standing at
the window, looking out. His mother said, "What's wrong,
Jackson?"

"Nothing."

"I know something is wrong, and your father knows
something is wrong. I am not leaving this room until I find
out what it is."

He suddenly realized that all the terrible, unspeakable
pain could be put into one simple word. "Alma."

"You're still worried about Alma?"

"Yes."

"I thought you'd gotten over that."

"No."

"You're worried that her husband is hitting her, is that
it?"

"I'm worried that he's going to kill her."

"Would it help if I went over there and talked to her?"

"No."

"She doesn't have to stay with him, you know. There
are places she can go. I'll find out who to contact. I saw
something in the newspaper just a week or so ago."

"Avondale."

To say the word was suddenly to be back in the car,

parked beside the road, clutching the steering wheel, listening to Alma ask to be taken home. His nose began to run, as it had then.

His mother did not speak. Jackson knew she was beginning to put the pieces together, to see how involved he was, how much he cared about Alma. The silence lengthened as she realized he would literally do anything—even steal her Cutlass Supreme—to help Alma.

"All right, now. Listen to me." She came over and turned him around. "There is nothing you can do to help Alma. Nothing! Do you realize that? There is nothing you can do." She pronounced each word as carefully as if it were a command.

"I know that."

"If he is hitting her—"

"It's not *if*."

"All right, then, it's a matter for the police."

"She won't go to the police."

"I will talk to her."

"Mom, she doesn't want you to know. She'll think I told. She—"

"I am going to talk to Alma. Period."

His mom turned and went into the living room. He could hear her flipping through the phone book. He could have called out the number—he had dialed it so often—but he did not want to have even that much to do with the arrangements.

"Alma, this is Kay Hunter, Jackson's mother." There

was a pause. "I want to talk to you. Would you rather I
came over there, or do you want to come here."

There were no other choices. His mother's natural talent for firmness had been perfected in stewardess school,
and Jackson knew Alma didn't stand a chance.

There was a pause. Then his mother said, "Fine, three
o'clock," and she hung up the phone.

Three O'clock, Four

"I want to talk to Alma alone," his mother said.

"I'll stay in my room."

"No, Jackson, I want you out of the house. Go over to Goat's."

"I won't eavesdrop, I just—"

"No! You are out of this, Jackson. Alma is no longer a concern of yours. Do you understand me?"

"I can't stop being concerned just because you order me to."

"I am not ordering you not to be concerned about Alma. I would be upset if you didn't care. What I am saying is that you are no longer involved in any way in the trouble between Alma and her husband. I want you to go to Goat's, and that is final."

This was the first time in his life his mother had ordered him to go to Goat's house. For years she had thought Goat crude because one time when she was giving a dinner party, Goat had come into the dining room, seen the table set for company, and said, just to be funny, "Oh, how thoughtful. Your mom has put little *handkerchiefs* by each plate in case the guests have to blow their noses." Then he had picked up a napkin and pretended to blow his nose. Unfortunately, at that very moment Jackson's mother had appeared in the doorway, and that had made Goat so nervous he actually did blow his nose in the napkin.

Jackson imagined that Goat no longer seemed like such a bad influence to her, because now her own son was a car thief.

He went into his room and got his jacket. He took a long time doing this, even though he knew he couldn't make getting his jacket last until three o'clock.

"All I wanted was to see how she looks, if she's all right," he said to himself.

"No," his mother answered from the living room.

"Will you at least tell me about it?" he asked on his way to the front door.

"No."

"Mom."

"No!"

He opened the door. He stared at the doorknob because

he knew from past experience how much his mother liked eye contact when she was talking to someone. "So, when am I allowed to come home?" he asked the doorknob.

"Five o'clock."

"Thank you very much."

Neither the doorknob nor his mother answered.

Jackson stood out on the corner, behind the mailbox. He wanted to get one last look at Alma.

As he stood there, hands jammed into his pockets, his hair hanging in his face, he told himself that actually it was a relief to be out of it all, to be on the outside, to be exiled to Goat's house. He told himself he was not ready to be an adult with adult responsibilities. He told himself he was lucky to be a child.

He looked at his watch. It was a quarter to three. Fifteen minutes to go.

One look, he told himself, just one last look, and he would be able to put the whole thing behind him. Suddenly he felt that he needed to do something boyish—fly a kite or whittle or make a model airplane. He looked at his watch.

Ten minutes to three.

He decided suddenly that he needed to be more like Goat. Goat had the right, easy-going attitude. Like, last year in school, their teacher, Miss O'Hara, who was Irish, wanted to have a big Saint Patrick's Day party. Everybody was supposed to wear green, and the person with the best costume would win a prize.

Everybody really went all out. They all had on green except Goat. He forgot. But he didn't go around begging, "Give me something green, please, somebody give me something green."

At the last moment, right before the class voted, he just very casually stuck two green Flair pens up his nose and won the prize.

Seven minutes to three.

Years ago, when Alma baby-sat for him, he remembered, she always came early. "I just couldn't wait to see my Cracker" was the reason she always gave. Maybe she would be early today and he could go on to Goat's. He would tell Goat, "My mom knows." That would be a relief also. Then Goat would stop asking if he could get the car. He imagined the conversation:

"Your mom knows we drove to Avondale?"

"She knows I did."

"But not me?"

"No."

"Whew."

Jackson looked at his watch. Five minutes to three.

The watch was a present from his dad. It was the third watch his dad had given him—a quartz. Maybe it needed a new battery. Time passed slowly on every watch his father had ever given him.

Four minutes to three.

When his dad gave Jackson the watch, he said, "You vant to know about vatches? I'll tell you about vatches.

Here's the story behind vatches. A clockmaker once made a little tiny clock. Und his vife said, 'It's stupid to haff such a little tiny clock. It vill get lost.' Und de clockmaker said, 'Not if you vatch it.' Und the clockmaker's vife said, 'You vant me to vatch the vatch?' Und the clock-maker—"

Jackson glanced down at his watch.

Five minutes past three! Alma was five minutes late!

He'd never known Alma to be late for anything. One time she'd told him, "I can't stand to be late. I'm always afraid I'll miss the best part of something. I am always the first person at a party, the first person at church. I used to even be early for school, and the only thing I liked about school was recess." It wasn't like Alma to be five minutes late.

And Jackson knew then that Alma wasn't coming.

The Accident

Even though Jackson was sure Alma was not coming, he kept standing behind the mailbox. No other option was open to him. He couldn't go back in the house until five o'clock, and he couldn't go on to Goat's house. He was nailed to this spot as surely as someone under a spell. He felt that only the sight of Alma coming down the street, her hair swinging in the wind, would free him.

By three-thirty his position was becoming uncomfortable. A woman across the street had started looking out the window every few minutes. He was trying not to look suspicious, but, as usual, he knew that only made him look more suspicious.

The woman's face—there it was again—was like every face he had seen spying at him from a window, mean and old. Maybe people bought special masks for the purpose.

"Clerk, I'd like to see something in a mean old mask."

"Of course, madam, you must be planning to spy on someone out your window."

The woman disappeared and Jackson wondered idly if she had gone to call the police.

"Well, it's like this, Officer," he could say, "the reason I have been standing behind this mailbox for an hour is because I am taking part in a survey to count the number of people using mailboxes. You see, it is impossible for the post office to estimate the number of people mailing letters from the number of letters in the box. You see, some people mail two letters, and some ten. It is even possible for two people to mail the same letter by . . . Yes, I could come to headquarters and repeat that to the sergeant."

Or, perhaps, "Well, it's like this, Officer. I have a friend who bet me a dollar I couldn't stand by this mailbox for an hour without somebody calling the police. In fact, my friend might well be the one who called you. Did he sound sort of like a mean old woman and did he—"

At that exact moment, ten minutes to four, his mother's car shot out of the apartment building's garage. He had never seen his mother drive this way even when she was late for a flight. He broke off his thoughts and leaped out from behind the mailbox.

"Mom! Where are you going?"

She did not even glance in his direction. He ran down the sidewalk after the car. He was yelling at the top of his lungs. "Mom!"

He cut into the street, which was a sure way to stop her. She always worried about him crossing the street. But now she did not even glance in the rearview mirror.

"Wait for me! Mom! Where are you going? Mom, wait!"

The silver Cutlass Supreme picked up speed, turned the corner practically on two wheels, and disappeared from sight, leaving Jackson standing in the middle of the road.

Jackson had run less than half a block, but for some reason he was out of breath. It was the surprise, he thought—no, the shock of seeing the Cutlass shoot out of the garage like a fire truck. There was only one place his mother could be going at that speed—to Alma's house. He ran back to the apartment.

His bike was in the downstairs hall, Day-Glowing quietly in the dark recess behind the stairs. He pulled it out, kicked up the stand, and was on the seat while the front door was still open.

He burst out of the building and rode down the steps like somebody in a motorcycle movie. He hardly felt the jarring jolt from the five steps. He pedaled down the walk, off the curb, and into the street.

Jackson had never been much of a speed demon on wheels—Goat used to call him "the Neon Turtle"—but now he bent forward like a racer. Hunched over the handlebars, he pedaled as if his life depended on it.

Houses streaked past; cars honked as he swerved past them; brakes squealed as drivers stopped short of hitting him. His only worry was what had happened at Alma's house to send his mother racing from the apartment.

Normally it was a twenty-minute ride to Alma's street, but Jackson made it to her corner in twelve. In the same fast way, he took the corner, sat back on the seat, and coasted the rest of the way. His mother's car was nowhere in sight.

He braked at the garage; the doors were shut. He went up on the sidewalk. There were no lights on in the house. The only thing to indicate either place was occupied was a line of baby clothes in the sideyard, the terry-cloth jumpsuits and tiny jeans limp in the still afternoon air.

Jackson rested on his bicycle and wondered what had happened. He had been so sure his mother would be here.

He had even imagined an ambulance in the driveway, Alma being carried out on a stretcher. He had imagined exactly the way her pale, unconscious face would look. He had imagined everything. The shock was finding nothing.

He dropped his bike and walked slowly up the walk to the house. He peered in through the front window.

He drew in his breath at what he saw. It did not look like Alma's living room. It was as if an indoor tornado had struck within the walls.

He cupped his hands around his face so he could see

better. Alma always kept everything tidy. "Cracker, I love my house. I can't stand to have one single thing out of place," she had told him.

Now, chairs were upended. Magazines on baby care and homemaking were all over the floor. Plants were overturned, the dirt spilled onto the carpet.

And everywhere there were Barbie dolls, thrown from the bookcase, lying in stiff-legged awkwardness, their outfits, shoes, hats, nurse's capes, scattered as if by the wind. There was something in the scene that sickened Jackson. It was as if he were looking at the site of a real battle, seeing the bodies of real people instead of—

A voice behind him said, "If you're looking for Alma and the baby, they aren't here."

Jackson spun around. He recognized the next-door neighbor.

"Where are they?"

"I think there was an accident. Some woman in a silver car took them to the hospital."

Jackson came to the edge of the porch. He held on to the railing for support.

"Who was hurt? Was it Alma? Was it the baby?"

He waited without hope for the answer. For the first time in his life, his throat, mouth, and nose were painfully dry.

"It looked like both of them was hurt to me," she said.

That Man

"You'll have to excuse me," the woman said. She crossed the street to tell another neighbor about the accident.

Suddenly it seemed to Jackson that his life had fallen into a terrible cycle. He was trapped somewhere, caught in a spell. Then he was sent hurtling to another space, where, again, he remained trapped in a spell.

The next cycle would be one of those wild, hurtling dashes. At the moment, however, he was unable to move.

He sank down on the cold steps.

"I knew something was going to happen," the neighbor across the street was saying. "It's that husband of hers." She shook her head. "The things I've heard."

"Tell," her friend said.

"Well, this was about a week ago. I was raking the leaves over by their fence and their window was open and . . ." She lowered her voice.

Jackson was grateful not to have to hear the rest.

He had no idea how long he sat there. It was one of those tricks of time. The sun got lower in the sky. The shadows lengthened. The afternoon darkened. And yet still, somehow, it was the exact same moment.

He looked up. The women had gone into their houses. The street was deserted.

With a sigh he got to his feet. He was stiff—he had been here that long, anyway, long enough to stiffen. Rip Van Winkle Junior. He walked to his bicycle, picked it up, got on. Like somebody from another century, on this modern convenience for the first time, he pedaled shakily for home.

His mother's car was not in the garage. That did not surprise him. Somehow he had known it would not be there. He couldn't think of anything else to do, so he pedaled in his slow, old-man's way to Goat's house.

He arrived at the time Goat's mother least liked to see him—suppertime. The house smelled of meat loaf and potatoes, and Mrs. McMillan did not bother to hide her displeasure.

"Ralph's getting ready to eat, Jackson."

"I know. I need to see him, Mrs. McMillan."

Goat's mother gave him a hard look. Usually this look—

Goat called it her witch impersonation—caused Goat's friends to say, "Oh, never mind. I'll catch him at school tomorrow," and hurry down the walk to safety.

Jackson met her hard glance without blinking. She must have seen something in his face to let her know this was not one of the usual I-need-to-see-Goat occasions.

"Five minutes."

"Thank you."

Jackson walked down the hall to Goat's room. Rachel gave Jackson a dirty look from her bedroom as he passed. "And what was *your* cut from the illegal UNICEF collection?" she sneered.

Jackson held up his hand, making a zero with his fingers.

"Huh!"

Jackson went into Goat's room. Just entering Goat's room brought Jackson a little comfort. Goat's mother had announced weeks ago that she would not clean his room until he picked up his things. "She's serious, too, pal, so do you realize what this means?" he had asked Jackson. "This means I can have everything exactly the way I want it—on my floor. I'll never have to open a drawer again for the rest of my life."

Goat was lying on the bed, reading, as content as a king in a castle. When he looked up, he could see instantly that something was wrong. "What's happened?"

Jackson blurted it out as he crossed the room—the expected visit of Alma, the sudden departure of his mother, his own mad dash to Alma's, the accident, his fears.

Goat said, "You want me to call the hospitals?"

Jackson sank down on the bed, his knees weak with relief. "Would you?"

"Sure. I did this last New Year's Eve because my mom thought my dad had been ın an accident. See, my mom had refused to go to a party with my dad because he had already had five martinis and he drove off without her and didn't get to the party. My mom found that out because she called the party to tell the host not to let him have any more booze and he wasn't there. My mom was pacing the floor and pacing the floor and I called all the hospitals and found out he wasn't there." Goat got the phone book. "And do you think she was grateful? She said, 'If you come in this room one more time, I am going to swat you.' "

He turned to the Yellow Pages. "Your mom probably took her to Saint Mary's because that's the closest." He dialed the number. "By the way, what's her last name?"

"Alton."

"Yes, this is Ralph Alton," he said into the phone. "My sister, Alma, was brought into the hospital—the emergency room—about four o'clock, she and her baby, and I wanted to inquire about their condition."

He looked at Jackson. "She's switching me to Patient Information."

"Hello, this is Ralph Alton. My sister, Alma, and her baby were brought in about four o'clock. They were in an accident." There was a pause while Goat waited, then listened. "Thank you."

He hung up the phone.

"She's been admitted. The baby has, too, but they won't give me any information."

"What does that mean?"

"That means," he said, and his face was suddenly long and sad, "that things are not very good."

Room 2002

Jackson stood outside Room 2002 trying to get the courage to go inside. He was holding his bouquet of flowers so hard the leaves were crushed. The flowers trembled in the green florist paper.

His mother had said, "I don't think you should go until she's had a few days to recuperate."

"I want to see her."

"She doesn't want you to. She's very self-conscious about the way she looks."

Alma, he knew now, had broken ribs, a punctured lung, a broken cheekbone, broken teeth, a broken wrist, and facial lacerations. Nicole had a concussion.

"I want to see her."

"You could call her, it's Room 2002, and then later—"

"I want to see her."

And yet here he was outside the door, leaning against the wall, trying to make himself strong enough to go inside. He knew now that what he had been telling his mother was "I *have* to see her," rather than "I *want* to see her," two entirely different matters.

He closed his eyes the way he used to do when he plunged off the board in diving class, and opened them inside the door.

"Oh, Cracker," Alma said. She put up one hand to shield her face from him. "I didn't want you to come."

He got it right this time. "I had to."

He walked toward the bed. Even if Jackson had been actor enough to keep the horror from his face, he would have been too affected to do so. He would not even have known it was Alma. Even her voice was different.

"I should have gone when you told me," Alma said.

One side of her face was so swollen Jackson could not even see her eye. Her lips were puffed. Her arm was in a cast. Every word she spoke was an effort.

"You didn't know."

He had made it to the edge of the bed now. He looked down at her fingers coming out of her cast. Ringless, swollen, even they were no longer familiar.

"I should have gone."

"Yes." He swallowed and said again, "You didn't know." He laid his limp bouquet on the table.

"I walked down to see Nicole a little while ago," Alma said. "Did you get to see her?"

"No."

"She looks so little and helpless."

Jackson cleared his throat. "Mother said the doctor thinks she's going to be all right."

"That's what the nurses say, but why hasn't she opened her eyes?"

"I don't know." He paused, desperate to think of something that would make her feel better. He blurted out, "They arrested Billy Ray."

"I know."

"What happened, Alma?" He had not meant to ask the question, his mother told him not to, but he could not hold it back.

"Just about what you'd expect. Billy Ray went crazy when he found out I was going to your mother's. He overheard the conversation on the garage extension."

"Don't talk about it if it makes you feel bad."

A tear somehow squeezed out of that swollen, unseen eye. Jackson felt the pinch of tears in his own eyes. His nose began to run.

"Billy Ray came in the house." She began to recite it. "I was standing by the TV. I was trying to decide whether to bring Nicole or leave her at Billy Ray's mother's house.

"Billy Ray came in and I turned around and without

any warning he hit me. He hit me here." She lifted her hand needlessly to indicate the side of her face. "He hit me with a wrench, Cracker, and he hit me so hard I don't remember anything else. I don't remember the ribs or the wrist or anything.

"I dropped Nicole, Jackson. That's the last thing I remember. I dropped her on the floor. In my nightmares I'm still dropping her. I guess I won't ever be able to forget that."

"You couldn't help it."

"If I had gone when you told me to . . ."

"Don't blame yourself."

"I'll blame myself for the rest of my life."

There was a silence, and then Alma said in a voice that made an effort to be cheerful, "Billy Ray's mother came to see me, did your mother tell you?"

"No."

"She was real nice. She said that on the way over here she was planning to ask me to give Billy Ray a second chance, but after she saw me—she didn't know about the wrench—after she saw me she changed her mind. She said, 'Alma, get away from him as fast as you can.' She said, 'I hate to say this about my own son, but he ought to be locked up.' "

"I agree."

There was another pause, and Alma made another attempt at good spirits. "Your mom's been so good to me. I'd be dead right now if she hadn't come and got me."

"She cares about you."

"I didn't use to think so."

"Everybody thinks that about my mom."

"She called that place in Avondale and the lady came and talked to me, did she tell you?"

"Yes."

"The lady was real nice. I wish I'd talked to her earlier. I would have left Billy Ray sooner if I had. She said that if your husband hits you, he's going to keep on doing it. He's not going to stop, no matter how many promises he makes. And the only way to stop him is to get out."

She looked at Jackson. "Just as soon as Nicole and I get better, we're going to Avondale." She tried to smile— her mouth went up on one side. "Will you come see me, Cracker?"

Jackson thought that the two halves of her face showed exactly what was going on inside her—half of her had been hurt so bad it would never be the same, but the other half still hoped for something good.

Smiling back at Alma was one of the hardest things he'd ever done in his life, his adult life, because it seemed as if he had stood outside the door a boy, then closed his eyes, walked inside Room 2002, opened them, saw Alma, and became a man.

"I'll come," he said.

Waiting for
Whale Imitations

Jackson was unlocking the door to the apartment when the phone started ringing inside. He dropped his books, yanked the door open, and rushed inside. He grabbed the phone off the hook, yelled, "Hello?"

Goat's voice said, "Hi, it's me."

"Oh."

"Well, you don't have to sound so disappointed. Who did you expect—the Pope?"

"Alma."

"I thought she was all right."

"She is, but the baby isn't."

"Oh." Goat had made an honest effort to sound concerned, but his voice began to rise with enthusiasm. "Guess what. Percy Gill has agreed to do his whale imitations!" He paused to give Jackson's excitement a chance to rise, too. "Come over as fast as you can. He already did one— a whale who has to go to the bathroom and Fellini won't excuse him. It broke us up."

"Maybe later."

"What do you mean later? Later it'll be over. Percy only gets in the mood to do whale imitations once a year. It's like a surfer when the surf's up. You don't wait. You come. I couldn't believe it when he agreed. This is a once-in-a-lifetime opportunity."

Jackson hesitated.

"Jackie, there's nothing like this for laughs. He even takes requests. 'Imitate a whale who has to wear his sister's bowling shoes in the tournament,' you call, and he does it. You got to see it to believe it."

"I don't think I can make it."

"It's your loss, pal."

"I know."

Jackson hung up the phone and sat down on the chair. He was genuinely torn. He wanted badly to see Percy Gill do his whale imitations. It was one of those things people are always bragging about. "You missed it, pal, Percy did his whale imitations." According to everybody, Percy doing his whale imitations was the funniest thing in the world. Jackson could have used a laugh right then.

He kept sitting there. However, he had been to see Alma again the day before—it had been four days since the accident—and Nicole still had not opened her eyes.

Alma had said, "You know what I've been thinking about, Cracker?"

He said, "No."

Alma was sitting on the edge of the bed in one of his mother's bathrobes. She said, "I've been thinking about this dog we had when I was little. Her name was Daisy, Cracker, and she had puppies. It was her first litter, and there were three of them. One was white and fuzzy and one was brown with white spots and one was black and brown and looked like a German shepherd.

"You know what? Later somebody told me that a litter of puppies can have several fathers, which I believed after seeing these three. Anyway, Daisy was a wonderful mother, but when the puppies got to be six weeks old, my mom started taking them away, one by one, and giving them to neighbors.

"She'd have to trick Daisy to get her out of the box, and Daisy would come back and see that a puppy was gone, and she would get frantic. She was just like a human mother. And the last one—it was the spotted puppy, which nobody wanted because it had such short legs—well, when she came back and it was gone, too, it was the saddest thing you ever saw in your life."

Alma started crying then. Tears had been rolling down her cheeks ever since she started the story of Daisy's puppies, but now she began to sob, terrible inward sobs that she swallowed like bad medicine.

"Don't think about it," he said.

"I can't help it, Cracker. I wish we hadn't taken them away. I really do. If I had known then what it was like to lose a baby, well, I never would have done it."

"You aren't going to lose Nicole."

"Do you really believe that?"

He nodded.

"That makes me feel better. You're always right."

"Not always."

"You know what I wish? I wish I could see Sister Rose. You probably don't remember her, but one time we went over there—"

"I remember."

"—and she told me I would marry Billy Ray but I would be sorry."

"I remember."

Suddenly her tears stopped. She looked hopeful for the first time since the accident. "Do you think you could find her, Cracker? Do you think you could ask her about Nicole getting well? She'd know."

"I could try," he said.

"You wouldn't mind? It wouldn't be too much trouble?"

"No."

"Oh, Cracker, you are the only person in the world that would do that for me. If it wasn't for you, I would just give up."

So that was why he sat on the chair without moving. He could either go over and see Percy Gill do whale imitations or he could get on a bus—which bus had it been?—and try to find Sister Rose. He could sit once again in that dim, feral parlor with the cats stalking around him, go into the dining room, and ask the question "Is Nicole going to get well?" He had no choice, really.

He picked up the phone book. He was wondering whether to look under Sister Rose or fortune-tellers when the phone rang. "Hello?"

"This is your operator. Will you hold for long distance? Idi Amin is on the line."

He said, "Hi, Dad."

"You didn't let me finish. You ought to at least let me finish."

"Go ahead."

"No, it wasn't that good, anyway. So, how are you?"

"Better."

"The reason I'm calling is that I can come next weekend—I just worked it out, and I'd like to see you. What do you think?"

"Fine."

"I'll call your mom tonight and work out the details."

"Great."

"See you then."

Jackson expected him to sign off like Liberace or Porky Pig—"Th-th-th-that's all, folks"—but he didn't. This time he just said good-bye like a normal person.

Jackson turned to the S's, and the phone rang again. "Hello?"

"Cracker."

He held the phone tighter so he wouldn't drop it if the news was bad. "Yes, it's me."

"I got good news." Alma's voice quivered with tears. "She opened her eyes."

"Oh." Now he dropped the phone out of relief. He pulled it back up by the cord. "Oh, I am so glad."

"I didn't get to see it, but the nurse swears it's true. They think she's going to be all right, Cracker. They think she's going to be fine."

He said again, "I'm so glad." It was something he had been wanting to say for so long that he didn't want to stop.

"I got to go. I want to be there the next time she does it. Tell your mom."

"I will."

He hung up the phone, grabbed his jacket, and ran out the door. He got on his Day-Glo bike and rode out of the building. He was getting good at taking the steps now.

He rode to Goat's in record time and flung open the front door without knocking. He ran downstairs.

There was a crowd in Goat's rec room. Percy Gill was in the middle, standing on the piano bench.

Someone called, "Percy, do an imitation of a whale who smells something bad and is trying to find out who caused it."

And Percy Gill, on the piano stool, actually became a

whale smelling something bad and wondering who had caused it.

Someone made room for Jackson on the floor and he sat. He was glad to be back in society.

On the Road Again

"Let's see, Jackson, do you want to drive, or do you want me to?" Jackson's father asked.

His father was home for the weekend, and he and Jackson and his mom were driving Alma to Avondale.

In the past day and a half, his father had made Jackson tell him every detail of his drive to Avondale. He had made him tell it over and over, and he had laughed so hard with each telling that he had to wipe tears from his eyes.

"You are encouraging him," Jackson's mom had warned. "It is no laughing matter."

But Jackson's father wouldn't listen. He'd say, "Tell

your mom the part about Goat running the red light and almost hitting the mail truck. Listen to this, Kay. This boy could go on television as a comedian."

Jackson opened the door to the back seat. "No, you go ahead and drive," he told his dad. "As you know, I've already been this route."

"Well, if you're sure you don't need the experience . . ." He slipped into the front seat, started the car. "I can remember my first drive. It was a short one, approximately five feet."

"I wish you wouldn't tell him these things," his mom said. "He and Goat get into enough trouble without you putting ideas in his head."

"I was nine years old," his father went on, undaunted, "and I was planning to drive my father's car around the block. It was an emergency situation. See, this friend of mine, Frankie Wynette, was having a party and Frankie had not invited me."

"Why not?" his mother asked.

"Well, actually, it was Frankie's mom who had not invited me, and I think it had something to do with the fact that I had made Frankie a parachute out of a pillowcase and persuaded him to jump off the garage to test it.

"Anyway," his father continued, "I knew the guests would be playing games out in the yard, and so while they were childishly pinning the tail on the donkey, I would tool past in my father's car. I would honk the horn, give a superior wave, and return home.

"While I was sitting there, figuring how to start the car, unbeknownst to me, my mother pulled up behind me in her car. I turned the key, whipped it into reverse, stepped on the gas, and backed into my mother's car, knocking her and her groceries to the ground. See, she was just getting out of the car and—"

His mom burst out laughing in spite of herself. "Oh, I can just see her."

"Actually, it was not that amusing, Kay. It was Eastertime and my mother was loaded with eggs."

This made Jackson's mom laugh harder. "I know I shouldn't be laughing," she said, trying to stop, "but I can't help it. What did you do?"

"For once in my life, I did the socially correct thing. I burst into tears. 'Mom,' I blubbered, 'something terrible's happened to our car. I was just sitting there and all of a sudden it went into reverse. Mom, if you hadn't come up right when you did and stopped me with your car, I would have gone out in the street and been killed.' "

"And what did your mother say?"

"Exactly what she always said: 'I'm going to tell your father on you!' " He sounded so much like his mother that they all laughed.

"This is it," Jackson's mom said, and the laughter in the car faded. It was Alma's driveway, and even Jackson's father couldn't turn this situation into something amusing.

Alma and Nicole were on the porch, sitting in the swing. A police officer was standing on the steps to make sure that Billy Ray didn't do anything to keep Alma from packing and leaving.

Alma hurried down the steps, carrying Nicole with her good arm. Her bad arm, in the cast, touched Nicole's back for extra support. The officer followed with two suitcases, three shopping bags, and the umbrella stroller. Jackson's father got out to open the trunk.

"Oh, I'm so glad you're here." Alma was trembling with relief. "I kept telling myself nothing could go wrong, with the officer here and everything, but I won't feel right until we've gone. I just don't know what I would have done if Billy Ray drove up."

"He knows not to do that, ma'am," the officer said.

Jackson's mother said, "It's natural to be nervous. But you're safe now. Nothing can happen."

"I hope not." Alma got into the back seat beside Jackson. "At least I don't have to get down on the floor this time." She laughed, nervously glancing out the window at the closed doors of the garage.

"Thank you for your help, Officer," Jackson's mother said.

"Have a safe trip," he called back.

Jackson's father backed the car out of the driveway. He said, "By the way, Kay, did I tell you she's going to the Fiji Islands?"

"Your mother?"

"It's a sort of senior citizens' swinging singles cruise, and . . ."

Instead of listening to his father's story, his mom's laughter, Jackson glanced at Alma. She was taking one last look at the house, and in her face was all the sadness of somebody saying a final good-bye. Jackson thought that immigrants must have looked like that as their boat pulled away from the home shore. She held Nicole up for one last look.

"Say good-bye, Sunbeam." She waved Nicole's hand awkwardly at the darkened house, the closed garage.

"I'm not even going to think about how it used to be," she said resolutely.

"You shouldn't."

"I'm going to think about how things are going to be."

Yet Jackson knew she had to be remembering the old times, because that was what he was doing. He found himself thinking about things he had not thought of in years—like the picnics they had had behind the garage. He was the slowest eater and suddenly Billy Ray would say, "Jackie, quick! Look over there!"

"Where?"

And when Jackson looked back, his sandwich would be missing, hidden under Billy Ray's shirt or behind his back.

"Don't fall for that!" Alma would laugh, retrieving the sandwich. "Next time he tells you to look, don't do it!"

And their wedding—it, too, had taken place in the field behind the garage. Jackson was ten years old and the only person present in a suit and tie. Alma had made up her own wedding vows, and she had been so worried she would make a mistake that she had called Jackson up on the phone again and again to practice reciting them. As she spoke them there, that fall afternoon, he had known them so well that his lips moved with hers.

He could probably still remember the vows. *I, Alma, who have loved you, Billy Ray, for five years with all my heart, do hereby promise to keep on for the rest of my—*

"Did you notice anything different about me?" Alma asked abruptly.

"What?"

She showed him her hands. "No rings. Remember all the rings I used to wear?"

"Yes."

"Remember you used to try them on?"

"Yes."

"Well, rings are supposed to make you remember. So I said, Alma, no more rings."

They had turned the corner now. The house, the garage, the field were behind them.

She wiped her eyes and said, "You're just going to have to excuse me, Cracker, because I'm going to cry a lot on this trip."

"That's all right."

"I promised myself I'd be brave, but everywhere I look I see a memory. Like I washed our clothes right there at that Laundromat before Billy Ray got me a Kenmore washer for my birthday. And we played putt-putt golf there one month before Nicole was born and I was so big

I couldn't see my ball to hit it." She swallowed. "When we get to Avondale, where there aren't any memories, I'll be fine."

"I know."

In the front seat his mom laughed again, and Alma said, "Your father is funny." Jackson knew she was probably wondering, as everyone else did, why his mother had ever divorced him.

"I know" was all he could tell her.

The drive, which took forever when Jackson was steering, sped past in one long, smooth glide. They were already at the spot where Alma had made him pull over, where she had threatened to get out of the car and walk back to Billy Ray if he didn't turn around. Jackson remembered getting out of the driver's seat, doing the do-si-do with Goat in front of the car.

"I'm sorry, Cracker," she said, "I'm going to cry again."

"That's all right."

She looked down at Nicole. "We're going to be happy, though, Gumdrop. I can't help crying, but I promise we're going to be happy."

The Non-Anonymous Letter

The letters came on Thursday. They were the only two letters in the mail that day, so it seemed to Jackson when he took them out of the mailbox that they had been delivered by something more special than the post office.

The letters were in pink envelopes with gardenias on the flap. One was addressed to his mom and one to him. The handwriting was the same.

Jackson took the letters into the apartment. He put his mom's on the coffee table and sat for a moment on the sofa, holding his.

Alma had been in Avondale two weeks, and not a day had gone by when he had not thought about her. He understood now the stories he had read about children whose loyalties are torn between parents. He had not even been torn between his mother and father during the divorce in the way he was now torn between what Goat called sympathetically "your two mothers."

Jackson worked his thumb under the flap and lifted it. The letter inside was on sheets of notebook paper. He unfolded them with care.

"Dear Cracker," the letter began.

Without thinking, he pulled a tissue from the box on the coffee table and held it to his nose.

> *Nicole and I are doing all right. Nicole has a new tooth and I have three.*

When Billy Ray hit Alma, three of her teeth had been knocked loose. She had been so sensitive about it that Jackson's mom had paid the dentist's bill herself.

He read on.

> *I am getting so I can stand to smile at myself in the mirror again.*
>
> *I have got a job working in a day nursery. I look after the babies. It is a good job because Nicole gets to be around other babies, and I don't have to be away from her, the way I would if I was a waitress. There's not a single baby in the nursery that I don't love.*

He turned to page two.

> *I think about you a lot, Cracker, and the way we used to be. Maybe what I'm going to say won't make any sense to you right now, but you are the only person I have to tell this to.*

He needed the tissues now.

> *A long time ago you and I went on the bus one day to see a woman that told fortunes.*

Sister Rose.

> *Remember, you were going to find her for me when Nicole wouldn't open her eyes?*
> *Well, that day Sister Rose told me two things. You've probably forgotten all about this, but she was right about one and she was wrong about one. She told me I would marry Billy Ray. She was right about that. The thing she was wrong about was that I would be sorry. And I never will be sorry about that because if I hadn't married him, I wouldn't have Nicole.*
> *When I think of it that way, Cracker, I don't feel as bad as I used to.*
> *Well, I have to go. The babies are waking up. Write me back.*

And it took a couple more tissues before he could read the last four words:

> *I love you, Alma.*

Up until this moment, Jackson had always had to lose something before he realized how much it meant to him. Like, he threw an old truck away one time, and the boy next door got it out of the garbage and started playing with it. Every day the boy would be out in the yard playing with Jackson's truck, and Jackson wanted it back so bad he wept.

And he used to have an old cap of his dad's. It was soft and brown and there was a button on top. Jackson used to sleep with that cap the way other kids sleep with their teddy bears.

One day his mom said, "You don't need this cap anymore, do you, Jackson? It's nothing but a rag." Some of Jackson's friends were there, and so he agreed she could throw it away, and he had missed that cap every single night of his life since.

So he felt he was lucky that right then, instantly, while the letter was in his hand, he realized its value.

Sure, he thought, the phone company tells you to reach out and touch someone, but he knew that was propaganda from the phone company. To be honest, he could hardly remember what his dad had said on the phone two nights ago. He had started like Bela Lugosi and ended like Johnny Carson, but Jackson couldn't remember much more.

But this letter. This letter . . . When he was fifty, he could read this letter and feel the same way he felt right this minute. When he was ninety, he could take out the letter, and his ninety-year-old nose would pour the same way his nose was pouring right now.

As long as he had this letter, he would never really lose Alma.

The phone started to ring.

Goat had told Jackson he would call if his mother found out what had happened in assembly. That morning, Goat had broken up the people sitting around him by telling a joke during the Pledge of Allegiance.

The principal had called Goat up on stage to teach him a lesson. "And just what was so amusing, Ralph?" the principal had asked.

Goat had confessed that he had been telling a joke.

The principal had said, "Perhaps you would like to share this joke with the assembly, Ralph."

Later, Goat had said, "I had to tell it, Jack. You heard him. It was a direct command from the principal!"

The trouble was that the joke was about a man who had taken an overdose of laxative, and the principal couldn't shut Goat up before he gave the punch line, which consisted of a sound effect.

The principal had told the assembly that Goat had used very poor judgment in repeating such a tasteless piece of filth. He made Goat apologize to everybody there, and then he announced he was going to call Goat's mother personally to inform her of the incident. He said he would like to call the mothers of everyone who had laughed at the tasteless piece of filth, but since that included everyone in assembly, it would be impossible.

"If he does call my mom," Goat had told Jackson on the way home from school, "I don't think he will, but if he does, there's always the chance I can receive the call myself and pretend to be my mom. Does this sound like her? 'I don't know what gets into that boy. His father and I have done everything but send him to reform school. We've already cut off his allowance for two years!' "

"It sounds like her."

"However, if he does get through," Goat went on thoughtfully, "then I will try to give you a short call so you won't be expecting me for supper. Stand by."

"I will."

Before Jackson picked up the phone, however, he went into his room and put his letter in the top dresser drawer, where, from now on, he would keep his most valuable possessions.

Then he picked up the phone.

He was not surprised to hear Goat's voice. "I am in deep trouble," he said.

Betsy Byars

was born in Charlotte, North Carolina, and lived there until her graduation from Queens College.

The mother of four, Mrs. Byars began writing books for children as her own family was growing up. She is the author of many books, including *The Summer of the Swans*, which received the Newbery Award.

Mrs. Byars now lives in South Carolina, where her husband is associated with Clemson University. She and her husband have traveled widely throughout the United States in pursuit of their interests in gliding and in antique airplanes.